This is no time for jokes! I just learned the terrible truth: *I'm a witch.* Here I thought I was just another teenager worried about making friends in my new school and how to get a guy I really like, Harvey, to notice me. That changed fast enough when my two aunts gave me a black pot and an old book, *The Discovery of Magic,* and my *cat* started giving me advice. I'm still trying to control my pointing finger and my runaway mind but between dead frogs, my worst enemy, Libby, and pineapples . . . but I'm getting ahead of myself.

My name's Sabrina and I'm sixteen. I always knew I was different, but I thought it was just because I lived with my strange aunts, Zelda and Hilda, while my divorced parents bounced around the world. Dad's in the foreign service. The *very* foreign service. He's a witch—and so am I.

I can't run to Mom—but *not* because she's currently on an archaeological dig in Peru. She's a mortal. If I set eyes on her in the next two years, she'll turn into a ball of wax. So for now, I'm stuck with my aunts. They're hanging around to show me everything I need to know about this witch business. They say all I have to do is concentrate and point. And I thought fitting in was tough!

You probably think I have superpowers. Think again! I can't turn back time, and I'm on my own when it comes to love. Of course, there are some pretty neat things I *can* do—but that's where the trouble *always* begins. . . .

**Sabrina, the Teenage Witch™ books**

#1 Sabrina, the Teenage Witch
#2 Showdown at the Mall

Available from ARCHWAY Paperbacks

# Sabrina The Teenage Witch™

A novelization
by
David Cody Weiss and Bobbi JG Weiss

"SABRINA, THE TEENAGE WITCH"
Based on Characters Appearing in Archie Comics

Developed for Television by
Jonathan Schmock

Pilot Episode
Teleplay by Nell Scovell
Television Story by Barney Cohen and Kathryn Wallack

"The True Adventures of Rudi Kazootie"
Written by Renee Phillips and Carrie Honigblum

"Dream Date"
Written by Rachel Lipman

AN ARCHWAY PAPERBACK
Published by POCKET BOOKS
New York   London   Toronto   Sydney   Tokyo   Singapore

This book is a work of fiction. Names, characters, places and incidents are products of the author's imagination or are used fictitiously. Any resemblance to actual events or locales or persons, living or dead, is entirely coincidental.

AN ARCHWAY PAPERBACK *Original*

An Archway Paperback published by
POCKET BOOKS, a division of Simon & Schuster Inc.
1230 Avenue of the Americas, New York, NY 10020

ISBN: 0-671-01433-1

First Archway Paperback printing June 1997

10  9  8  7  6  5  4  3  2  1

AN ARCHWAY PAPERBACK and colophon are registered trademarks of Simon & Schuster Inc.

SABRINA THE TEENAGE WITCH and all related titles, logos and characters are trademarks of Archie Comics Publications, Inc.

Front cover photo by Bob D'Amico

Back cover photo by Don Cadette

Printed in the U.S.A.

IL 5+

☆

# Prologue

☆

The Spellman sisters' old Victorian house stood in the middle of its block, looking little different from its neighbors in the small New England town. Moonlight dripped down its corner tower and cast deep shadows under its gables and intricate scrollwork. Ivy climbed a side wall, partially covering windows of the upper stories. A massive brick chimney, cold and unused on this warm autumn night, rose above the rooftop. But things are often not what they seem on the outside, and inside this house, life was about to change forever for those who lived there.

A book-lined study lay to one side of the grand staircase that rose opposite the front door. In the study, an antique clock began to chime, marking the deepest point of the night. The hollow sound echoed throughout the dark house.

*Dong . . . dong . . . dong . . .*

Two women tiptoed up the back staircase, their slippers making no sound on the blue floral carpet runner. The elder Spellman sister led the way, a red fringed shawl draped loosely over an Empire-cut olive nightgown. She wore her pale blond hair swept high on her head, and she carried an air of Renaissance gentility with her up the treads. Her name was Zelda, and her eyes glittered with joyful anticipation. She whispered to her sister, "It won't be long now, the minute we've been waiting for—midnight!"

*. . . dong . . . dong . . . dong . . .*

The younger Spellman climbed the stairs a little less gracefully than her sister. She was slightly stockier of body, and her shag-cut blond hair framed a face whose chipmunk cheeks and mischievous eyes belied her six hundred–plus years. She wore blue silk pajamas and moved with the impatience of a child. Her name was Hilda.

*. . . dong . . . dong . . . tunk!*

Hilda hissed a warning downstairs. "Salem! Stop messing with that clock!"

*"Mrrawwr!"* came a screech from below. Claws scrabbled across polished wood until they gripped carpet, and a streak of black velvet zipped up the stairs to the landing. The third nocturnal prowler, a large black Burmese cat, stopped for a quick tongue bath while waiting for the slower humans to catch up.

*. . . dong . . . dong . . . dong.*

2

The women paused at the bedroom door at the top of the staircase. Hilda started toward the door, but Zelda stopped her with a hand. "Her sixteenth birthday just started." She moved in front of Hilda and quietly opened the bedroom door.

Before her lay a bay-windowed room that combined Victorian style with touches of modern color and fabric. A brass sun pinned the drapery to the wall over the bed like a brooch. It reflected the reds and golds of the mute ballet being performed in the lava lamp on the nightstand. Ivy covered half of the stained-glass bay window. Dapples of moonlight crept through the ivy to dance on a single bed with its high carved headboard. A desk scattered with school supplies sat catercorner to the bed, and clothes spilled out of a closet next to the door. Salem sniffed at these and took up his customary station in the bay window.

In the center of the room a sleeping young girl shifted without waking, her blond hair sweeping back from her head to hang down, as her white cotton nightgown did, in the air some four feet above the bed.

Zelda clasped her hands together, thrilled. "Oh, Hilda, look," she cooed to her sister. "She's levitating! Right on schedule!"

Hilda's dimpled smile quirked into a wry smirk. "Let's wake her up and tell her she's a witch," she blurted, making a move toward the bed.

Zelda stopped her. "No," she said softly but firmly. "Let her sleep. She starts a new school

3

tomorrow. And besides"—Zelda's firmness melted into sentimentality—"the first levitation is special."

"Yeah," agreed Hilda, ruefully remembering how she'd bumped into walls while she slept, "but it gets old *real* quick!"

The sisters, caught up in their own reminiscences, gazed fondly at the sleeping girl. Zelda sighed. "I can't believe our niece is growing up. Wait till Sabrina finds out what new doors this opens for her."

"Wait till she finds out you still get zits when you're six hundred years old!" Hilda shot back.

Sabrina shifted slightly again, still not waking. Zelda tugged at Hilda's pajama sleeve. "Well, let's go before she wakes up."

Quietly they backed out of the bedroom. Zelda took one last look at the sleeping teenager floating above her bed and at the alert black cat who watched diligently from his cushion in the bay window. "So sweet, so innocent," murmured Zelda. "Just the perfect little witch."

# ☆
# Chapter 1

☆

$\mathcal{S}$abrina's bedroom by morning light was no little girl's idyllic resting place. It was a fashion battlefield. Clothes were strewn across the bed and the floor. The closet door hung open and tops, skirts, pants, and dismembered matching outfits tumbled out in a multicolored pile.

Sabrina stood in front of her full-length mirror, one foot in a sneaker and the other in a high-heeled shoe. It had taken her an hour, but she had finally settled on a purple satin top over black jeans and only had the shoes left to choose. She addressed the reflection of the cat in the mirror. "Which do you think, Salem?" Sabrina stood flat-footed on the sneaker foot. "Sneakers?" She shifted her weight to the other foot, lifting her up a good two inches. "Or high heels?" She shifted down again. "Sneakers . . ." Up again. "Or heels?"

Salem—the real cat, not the reflection—was contorted into a position a yoga master would envy. He had pointed his left rear leg toward the ceiling with the grace of a ballerina while he rotated his head 170 degrees to bite an itchy spot behind his knee. He paused from his grooming long enough to raise a sarcastic eyebrow at the whole dressing routine. Then he rolled over and went to sleep.

"Sabrina!" Zelda called from downstairs. "You'll be late!"

Footgear was still an undecided issue, but a panicked glance at the clock settled the affair. "Okay. Sneaker." Sabrina kicked the high heel into the closet and jammed her other foot into the other sneaker, wedging it in without untying the laces. She grabbed her backpack, which was stuffed with school supplies, and headed for the door. The mess on the floor caught her attention, and she remembered a splotch of black cat hair that had spoiled a white outfit that would otherwise have been perfect for today. She turned back, scooped Salem up from his sunny spot, and dashed downstairs, slamming the bedroom door behind her.

The Spellman kitchen was a warm spacious room that reeked of homeyness and comfort. Less formal than the dining room, it was the place of choice for meals during the still-in-nightgowns part of the day. The original massive brick fireplace had been converted into an alcove for a cast-iron gas stove and a modern refrigerator. Cast-iron cookware and copper pots hung from hooks set into the brickwork. A tile-topped island separated the cooking area from the breakfast set, which faced the French doors that led to the back porch and the yard beyond. Blue walls and ivory-white doors made the room bright and airy.

Hilda sat at the table, finishing a plate of toast and eggs. Brushing crumbs from her mouth as she heard Sabrina gallop down the stairs, she turned to greet her niece. Zelda glided out from behind the island to lead Sabrina to the table.

"Good morning," Sabrina said brightly, handing Salem off to Hilda.

Zelda beamed. "Happy Birthday, Sabrina! And many, *many* more to come." She walked over to the island, picked up a gaily wrapped box, and brought it back to the table. "I got you a little something."

Hilda grinned sheepishly at Sabrina. "Uh, that's from both of us—I just forgot to sign the card."

Zelda shot her sister a stern look but refused to allow herself to be sidetracked. She offered the box to Sabrina. "Hope you don't already have one," she said.

Sabrina took the box lightly, then tightened her grip at its unexpected weight. She removed the lid and lifted out her present—a cast-iron pot about eight inches in diameter, complete with an iron handle to hang it from. "A black pot," Sabrina said slowly, trying to be polite. "Actually, I don't already have one. Thanks."

"It's a cauldron," corrected Zelda.

Sabrina gave a strained smile. "Wow. Even better. I can"—she groped for words—"put my pens in it," she finished lamely.

"That's not what it's for," said Zelda. She took a breath, as if steeling herself for a difficult task. "Sabrina, we have something to tell you."

Sabrina was puzzled. Something was obviously going on.

"You see," Zelda began slowly, "there are two realms—the natural and the supernatural." Hilda, never big on patience, began fidgeting, anticipating another of her sister's long-winded explanations. "And it turns out that the immutable laws of physics—"

"You're a witch!" Hilda interrupted.

"What?" said Sabrina.

"You're a witch," Hilda repeated. She smirked at Zelda. "Now she knows."

Zelda looked at her sister with the irritated tolerance that only an older sibling could master. "Thank goodness *I* gave her the sex talk," she sighed.

Sabrina tried to refocus her aunts' attention. "What do you mean, I'm a witch?"

Zelda tried the patient approach. "I know it's a surprise. But you're not alone. I'm a witch. Hilda's a witch. And your father's a witch."

"And I suppose my mom's a witch, too?" asked Sabrina facetiously.

Hilda muttered, *"I* always thought so."

Zelda ignored her sister. "Actually," she said, "your mom's mortal. You see, that's why you're here . . . so we can teach you to use your magic."

Sabrina suddenly laughed. Still chuckling, she hefted her backpack and stood up. "You know, for a second there you almost made me forget about my first day of school." She walked to the French doors, opened one, and paused dramatically. "But now I've got to go catch a bus to take me to my doom." She left.

As Sabrina crossed the back porch, Salem ran ahead of her to perch on the railing and her aunts called after her.

"We can talk about this later," said Zelda. "Have fun at school."

"And don't make too many hand gestures!" shouted Hilda.

Sabrina scratched Salem's head and whispered to him conspiratorially. "My aunts try hard, but you have to admit they're pretty weird." Salem just stared at her with round golden eyes.

Sabrina was around the corner and out of earshot when the cat commented in a rich tenor voice, "You have *no* idea!"

Westbridge High School was a sprawling two-story pile of brick that looked less like a place of learning than a fortress designed to protect the teachers from the horde of laughing, chattering teenagers flowing into it. Sabrina felt dwarfed by all the bustle, the clamor, the total *newness* of everything.

And to top it off, she saw at once that her choice of footwear was a fashion mistake. Every female foot was clad in a high-heeled shoe and was clacking sharply on the aged linoleum. Not another sneaker in sight. Sabrina hid behind her open locker door, willing herself to become invisible.

Her effort didn't succeed. A trio of haughty cheerleader types raked Sabrina coldly with their eyes as they sauntered by. Their leader, a brunette with an attitude of silk over steel smiled scornfully. Then her lackeys both smiled similar smiles, as if sharing a secret joke, before their leader turned her back on Sabrina and led her troop away.

Punctured to the quick, Sabrina scuttled across the hall, holding her backpack low, as if hoping to hide the offending sneakers. She leaned against the doorjamb of her first classroom. Through the window of the door she saw a tall, gorgeous boy. A hunk. Firm-jawed and tousle-maned, he grinned as their eyes met. Sabrina felt herself starting to melt on the spot.

The mood was shattered when the teacher opened the door inward and hit the boy in the head with it. The teacher, a thin fellow who looked as if he'd sucked pickles for breakfast, beckoned Sabrina in. "Summer's over," he said, managing to sound cheerful and doomed at the same time. "Come on in."

Sabrina entered to find the room filled with stone-topped lab tables facing a battered oak desk and a blackboard beyond. The tables stood in two rows, each table set up with two dissection trays and four stools. Sabrina snagged an unoccupied stool and watched as the teacher wrote "Mr. Pool" on the blackboard in back-slanting letters.

"I'm Mr. Pool," he said, punctuating his name with an underlining slash of chalk on the blackboard. He turned and grinned sardonically at his students. "Now, I know you were hoping I'd spend the day mispronouncing your names, but instead, we'll jump right into sophomore biology."

Mr. Pool snapped a collapsible pointer out to full length and tapped at a diagram of a frog that hung on the wall. "The frog is a cold-blooded vertebrate. As we dissect this amphibian, we'll be looking for the kidneys—*(tap)*—the heart—*(tap)*—and my lost youth—*(tap).*" He looked relieved to hear a few halfhearted chuckles. Collapsing his pointer, he continued, "So if you'll each choose a lab partner . . ."

The room froze in silence. Following the first rule of teenage life, "Thou shalt not volunteer first," they shifted their heads slightly as each person waited for someone else to make the brave move.

Mr. Pool pursed his lips. "Or I could pair you off by height."

Feet shuffled as the students rushed to pair up.

"Thank you," Mr. Pool said with a sneer.

Sabrina looked across to the next table and recognized the hunk from the door scene. He looked back at her and, with another shy grin, said, "Hey, you wanna—"

"I'll be your lab partner, Harvey," chirped a brunette who suddenly materialized at the boy's elbow. Sabrina recognized her as the leader of the girls who had snubbed her in the hallway. Harvey looked confused for a second, then grinned good-naturedly at the cheerleader. "Sure."

Sabrina fumed. The interloper had snatched Harvey right out from under her nose! Sabrina was chewing over the things she *should* have said when she noticed a thin girl with a mountain of wavy red hair coming toward her. "Hi, I'm Jenny Kelly. Want to work together?"

Sabrina beamed with relief. "Yeah," she said. "That'll be great."

The two girls moved to unoccupied seats in front of a dissecting tray holding a spread-eagled frog. Mr. Pool began slouching up and down the aisles, glancing down at the dead frogs. "Now acquaint yourself with your frog," he lectured tiredly. "But we know how this story is going to end, so try not to get emotionally attached."

Jenny grinned and said to Sabrina, "Let's call our frog Tad. Tad Pole."

"Okay." Sabrina laughed. Then she added, "Hey, thanks for asking me to be your lab partner."

Jenny adopted an attitude of hard-won experience. "I was the new kid last year. I know what it's like."

"So," ventured Sabrina, "can I ask you a question? Do you ever feel that you don't fit in?"

"Only all the time," Jenny answered ruefully. "But I don't *want* to fit in. I researched it, and I found out that awkward people tend to be much more successful later in life. I look at Libby,"—she pointed over her shoulder at the cheerleader batting her thick eyelashes at Harvey—"and I see tragedy."

"What do you mean?" asked Sabrina, shocked. "She seems like the most popular kid in school."

"Exactly. She's peaking right *now*. It'll just be a long, sad, slow slide downhill from here."

A beaky face suddenly appeared between them. "Aw, look, girls," said Mr. Pool, pointing at the dissecting tray with mock dismay. "You've bored your frog to death. Slice and dice!" he ordered cheerily and moved on.

The girls returned their attention to the frog, and Sabrina made a face. "I hate doing this." She frowned. "If only there was some way I could bring these frogs back to life." She studied Tad closely, her finger circling its pale, formaldehyde-soaked body. "I think his heart is somewhere around"— she pointed—"here."

A tiny spark leaped from Sabrina's finger to the frog. The animal's dead skin flushed to a healthy green, and the heavy back legs began to twitch.

"Look!" Sabrina shouted. "Tad's alive! How'd that happen?" Tad rolled over onto his belly and performed a couple of test jumps.

Beside her, Jenny shrieked with glee and grabbed the frog just before it hopped off the table. "It's Frankenfrog! Hey, Mr. Pool, ours is still kicking!"

A giddy girl at the next table screamed, and Mr. Pool muttered angrily to himself as he came to inspect the frog. "Oh! Mike from Cadaver Shack is going to hear from me!"

Sabrina was still amazed and amused at the frog's resurrection when she walked into the nearest girls' room to wash the smell of formaldehyde off her hands. As intimidating as school seemed only an hour ago, things were, well . . . *hopping* now! With a renewed sense of confidence, she entered the lavatory . . .

And suddenly felt as if she'd entered a minefield. Standing in front of the two mirrors over the sinks were Libby and her cronies, who Sabrina knew from roll call were named Cee Cee and Jill. The sinks were littered with open compacts, dozens of tubes of lip color, and a boutique's worth of flavored lip gloss.

"I can't believe how *young* the freshmen look," Libby was saying as she preened. Her cohorts laughed their agreement. Their laughter abruptly stopped when Sabrina entered. Libby saw her in the mirror and turned, inquiring in a frosty voice, "May we help you?"

Sabrina tried to smile despite the subzero greeting. "I want to wash my hands." She held up her palms. "You know—frog juice."

Like an empress giving alms to a leper, Libby stepped to one side and gestured minimally toward the sink. Sabrina stepped forward and began washing her hands.

"You know," Libby began ultra-politely, "if you stink, I'm not sure it's fair to blame the frog." Jill and Cee Cee smothered giggles behind their hands.

A flash of irritation lit Sabrina from inside. Before she realized it, she retorted, "Well, at least I don't splash on aftershave to remind me of some boy who dumped me last summer."

Libby's jaw dropped, and her eyes sparked in sudden fury. "How'd you know that?"

Behind her, Jill and Cee Cee made keep-quiet motions with their hands and mouths.

"I-I don't know," Sabrina said, dumbfounded. Why *had* she said that to Libby? Even stranger, she knew that what she'd said was true. But *how* did she know? She groped for an answer. "My . . . incredible sense of smell told me?" That sounded lame even to Sabrina.

"Yeah, right," Libby said with a sneer.

Sabrina hastily dried her hands on a paper towel. "Well, gotta get going." She brushed past Libby. A flicker of spite made her toss in, "Smell you later."

Libby took up her station in front of the mirror, then reasserted her control of the situation. She pointed a finger commandingly at Sabrina. "Wait.

Don't come in here again. From now on, *you* use the *freaks'* bathroom." Then, in unison, she and her cronies turned back to their primping, dropping a wall of scorn between themselves and their new school-yard scapegoat.

Sabrina frowned. Then, mockingly imitating Libby's imperious gesture, she pointed her own finger, swooping it through the air to end in a jab at the brunette's back before she turned to leave.

Libby's yeep of panic made Sabrina turn back. As if with a will of its own, Libby's hand was moving a lipstick across her face in spastic little jerks, leaving carmine smears on her nose, cheeks, chin—everywhere but on her lips, it seemed. Libby was horrified but couldn't seem to stop her hand.

Sabrina ducked out of the rest room as fast as she could. Whatever surprises she'd expected from her first day at Westbridge High, they were nowhere near the weirdness that was happening.

What in the world was going on?

☆

# Chapter 2

☆

Hi, I'm home," called Sabrina as she bounced into the kitchen.

Silence.

"Where is everybody?" she called again.

Neither of her aunts was present to welcome her back after her first day of school, though they had promised to be there. Puzzled, Sabrina opened the door to the dining room.

Like all the other rooms on the ground floor, the dining room had a high ceiling and tall windows. Opposite the windows was a dark wood buffet topped by a hutch. Fresh-cut lilics sprouted from crystal and silver vases that bracketed an ivory carving of the three Graces. The table seated eight, plus a high-backed stool set at a corner. On the table was a frosted sheet cake with "Happy Birthday, Sabrina" inscribed in blue icing and bordered with yellow marzipan roses.

"Surprise!" shouted Hilda and Zelda, popping up from hiding. They hurried to Sabrina's side.

"Oh, look," Sabrina said with false cheerfulness. "A party . . . sort of," she trailed off, realizing that the only attendees were her aunts and the cat, who sat on the stool. He wore a cone of spiraling pink and purple foil on his head, and in front of him was a bowl of milk. "And look—you put Salem in a little party hat. That is *so* cute!"

The party may have been short on numbers, but Sabrina's aunts weren't going to let it fall short in festivity. They had dressed up for the occasion and laid the table with a fine Irish linen tablecloth. Hilda flounced over in her pale green Chinese silk blouse and guided Sabrina to the head of the table. But instead of a place setting, there was a polished wooden lectern before Sabrina's chair.

Zelda floated by, slim and sedate in an indigo sheath, and lifted an enormous book from the buffet. She showed it to Sabrina. "Here is a present from your father." She set the volume down on the lectern.

It was leather-bound, easily twenty inches tall, and nearly that wide. A rainbow of gemstones studded the corners of the cover and formed a circle in its center. A wide red satin bookmark looped from the spine through the book and out the bottom. "An old book. A black pot." Sabrina felt a little hurt, but she tried to make a joke out of it. "Doesn't anyone shop at the Gap anymore?"

That didn't get a rise out of her aunts, so Sabrina looked more closely at the book. Its title, *The Discovery of Magic,* was spelled out in ornate gilt lettering on the cover. "Why'd he give me this?" She opened the huge volume to the bookmark and examined the strange pictures and text.

The pages were much thicker than those in ordinary books. They were parchment—sheepskin scraped thin and rubbed smooth enough to write on. Or print on, Sabrina realized when she saw that the old-fashioned lettering was a form of type. And the illustrations were etchings or engravings.

And what they illustrated! There were diagrams of the human body with labels showing which parts were governed by which planets. There were astrological charts, tables of alchemical formulae, and lists of plants and their uses.

The page to the right of the bookmark bore a line engraving of a dapper warlock in an old-fashioned tuxedo and top hat. A scroll under the picture read, "Edward." That picture brought a rush of homesickness to Sabrina's heart. "That's why!" she said, answering her own question. "This old magician looks just like my dad!"

As she stared at it, the drawing shimmered and acquired depth. In a moment it was as if the book held a window that contained the small image of a living man. The warlock looked up at Sabrina and declared, "Surprise! It *is* your dad. Happy birthday, Sabrina!"

Now *that* was cool! She looked at her aunts and giggled, "Wow! Hallmark has really gone high-tech! Can he say anything else?"

"I'm not a hologram, honey," said Edward Spellman from the page in the book. "I'm just in a different realm."

Sabrina reflexively talked back to the illustration. "A different realm? I thought you were at the Toronto Midway Motor Lodge."

Edward's voice boomed out of the book. "Zelda! Hilda! Didn't you explain to Sabrina that she's a witch?"

"She doesn't believe us," Zelda countered defensively.

Hilda added, "Maybe this would be easier for her if we were wearing pointy black hats."

Zelda looked puzzled. "I don't even know where mine is."

"Not this again!" Sabrina stood up and slammed the book shut. She tried to be polite to her aunts. "Look, I know you went to a lot of trouble to set this joke up, so—ha-ha-ha. Now it's over."

"No," said Hilda, exasperated herself, "it's just beginning. You *are* a witch!"

"With real magical powers," Zelda chimed in. "And now that you're sixteen, you can use them." She quirked her face in wry amusement. "And you wanted something from the Gap!"

Sabrina still wasn't buying it. "So what are you

20

saying? That *I'm* not who I think I am? *You're* not who I think you are? And my father lives in a *book?*"

"Finally, she gets it!"

Sabrina threw her hands up in the air. "This is insane!" she snapped. "I'm going to my room. Come on, Salem." She stalked toward the door.

"Can you wait till I finish my milk?" drawled Salem.

Sabrina froze in the doorway, then spun back to stare at the cat, eye to eye. She shot a plaintive glance at her aunts. "Did the cat just talk?"

"Yes," Salem replied, almost in her ear. "And get this stupid hat off my head."

"Omigod!" Sabrina yelped and bolted for the stairs.

Zelda turned to her sister. "I think we'd better let her father handle this." She gestured at the book. "Ed . . .?"

The enormous book floated up from the table and hung for a moment in midair, then followed the teenager upstairs. When Sabrina reached her bedroom door the book was floating at eye level behind her.

At the sight of it, Sabrina screamed and leaped backward into her bedroom. The book followed. Sabrina grabbed it and slammed it down on her desk, then threw herself on the bed, putting as much space between herself and the book as possible.

"Sabrina! Open me up!" commanded her father's muffled voice from inside the book.

Sabrina cowered. "No!"

"We have to talk!" Then sternly, "Young lady, you open me up this instant!"

"No! I don't want to talk to a book!" Sabrina clapped a hand to her forehead, nearly in tears. "Oh, God! I'm talking to a book!"

It took a moment for her to calm down. Then, hesitantly, she slid off the bed and approached her desk. The book lay there, silent. With a trembling hand, Sabrina opened it to the page with her father's image. "I *can't* be a witch," she said plaintively. "Witches don't exist."

The illustration's face took on that look of firm insistence that Sabrina recognized all too well. If nothing else, this proved that it was her father, all right. "Honey, I know this is hard," Edward Spellman said gently, "but you have to accept it. You're not like other kids. You're special."

Sabrina moaned. "I don't want to be special—I want to be normal!"

"I understand. But . . . that ship has sailed."

"None of this makes sense," complained Sabrina. "I mean, all these years I thought you were traveling with the foreign service."

"I am. It's just a lot more *foreign* than you thought."

A sudden suspicion hit Sabrina. "And Mom? Has she *really* been digging for fossils in Peru?"

"Yes, she has."

"Then I want to go and live with her!"

"You can't. You see, there's a rule." Her father paused. "If you set eyes on your mother in the next two years, she'll turn into a ball of wax."

Sabrina's eyes bugged. "What?"

Edward shrugged. "It's the way they discourage mortal-witch marriages."

"Is that the reason you and Mom got divorced?"

"Nnno." He drew the syllable out, as if a simple no couldn't convey the complexity of the real story.

A glimmer of hope flickered inside Sabrina. "So do you think maybe you'll get back together?"

"Nnno. That's *another* ship that's sailed." Edward looked fondly up at his daughter. "You're going to be fine, Sabrina. Just take some time and think about all this. And if you *ever* need me"—he beamed mischievously—"I'm in the index to this book."

Edward Spellman's image flattened, grew grainy, and then became a line engraving once more. Sabrina stared at it for a long, long time.

The Spellman sisters were playing cards at the dining table. While Sabrina was in her room, they had gone ahead and cut the cake, taken portions, and moved the rest to the sideboard. Tea and cards had inevitably followed. Zelda had finished her cake and was working on her tea, but Hilda still had the remains of a second piece of cake on her plate, surrounded by a halo of crumbs. "I call!" announced Hilda, flashing her cards triumphantly at Zelda. "Five aces!"

"You cheat!" accused Zelda.

Hilda reacted with shock. "Do not."

"Do too!"

"Do not!"

"Okay," Sabrina interrupted, walking in and plunking herself into a chair. "I've talked to my dad . . . and I guess I believe I'm a witch."

"Good," snapped Hilda, happy to be proved right about something. "'Cause you are."

Zelda tactfully forgot the card game and turned her attention to her niece. "Hey, you know what? Let's try some magic." She got up and crossed to the walnut sideboard, where she picked up an orange from a chased silver fruit bowl.

Sabrina brightened immediately. "Can I turn a pumpkin into a Porsche?" she asked.

"Ooh, good one!" Hilda grinned.

"Let's start with the basics," Zelda suggested somewhat primly. She placed the orange in the center of the table, then directed the others about. "Sabrina, you stand right there." She indicated the head of the table. "Hilda, you stay there."

Zelda stood behind Sabrina and aimed her index finger at the orange. "Orange into apple. Now, concentrate and point. C'mon, try it."

Sabrina pointed her finger. Her jaw clenched as she concentrated. *Orange into apple, orange into apple, orange into—* The orange shimmered and lost shape, pulsing with light for a moment before suddenly stretching upward and growing bumps that turned into five-pointed bracts. Amazingly, a pineapple sat where the orange had been.

"Apple . . . pineapple," Zelda said encouragingly. "That's very close."

Hilda snorted with sarcastic humor. "No, it's not."

"Try again," Zelda suggested patiently, waving for Hilda to be quiet.

Sabrina raised her hand to point again, but then she snorted, letting it drop back to her side. "I feel stupid."

"You're lucky you don't have to wiggle your nose," commented Hilda.

With the ease of long practice, Zelda ignored Hilda's remark. "Try again," she prompted Sabrina, tossing another orange to Hilda to place on the table. "And *focus*. Orange . . . into apple."

Sabrina raised her hand again.

Nearly two dozen pineapples later, Sabrina gave up in frustration. Pineapples stood on almost every available surface in the dining room. They sat in ranks on the sideboard. They gracefully ringed the three Graces. Hilda had run several through a juicer.

"I'm not very good at this," Sabrina complained. "You told me the twenty-third time is the charm."

"You'll learn to control your magic," Zelda promised, smoothing back her niece's hair. "At the very least, you'll always be able to garnish a ham steak."

Sabrina was punchy with effort. An idea struck her, and she scurried around the table to where the cat sat on his special stool, watching the proceedings with the amused scorn only a cat could pull off. "One more try—Salem into apple!" Sabrina pointed.

"I think that's enough for one night!" Salem said hastily, his tail twitching.

"The cat's right," Hilda agreed. She twirled her hand in a circle. "Wrap it up. You have school tomorrow."

Sabrina slumped. "I'm a witch and I still have to go to school?"

"Mm-hmm," confirmed Zelda.

"Unfair!" Sabrina declared. Then her imagination kicked in. "Hey, maybe I'll turn Mr. Pool into—"

Hilda was quick to interrupt this line of thought. "Now, be careful pointing your finger at people. That could be dangerous." She waggled a finger at Sabrina.

"You're pointing at me." Tiredness made Sabrina sassy.

"*I* have the safety on!" Hilda smirked.

Her aunts were right. It was time for bed.

☆

# Chapter 3

☆

$S$abrina was floating peacefully over her bed when the alarm clock rang the next morning. She turned automatically to slap it quiet, waking up as she did so. As soon as she opened her eyes, however, her sleep-time levitation ceased and she dropped like a stone onto her bed. Apparently there were some drawbacks to being a witch.

When she skipped down the stairs to the kitchen an hour later, her aunts were perched on the island, pecking at bowls of pineapple chunks. It had only taken Sabrina forty-five minutes to decide on tan slacks and a black shirt with a gold snowflake print. She made a mental note to bug her aunts about fashion magic. Zelda smiled up at Sabrina as she entered. "Morning," she said.

"Morning," Sabrina said, smiling back.

"Pineapple?" Hilda offered by way of greeting.

Sabrina shook her head and sauntered across the kitchen to the refrigerator, which she opened to get a bottle of orange juice. Zelda raised an eyebrow at her niece's lazy pace. "You're going to be late," she warned.

Sabrina shot back a grin as she set the juice on the island. "So? I'm a witch. Can't I just turn back time?"

"Nuh-uh," Hilda answered around a juicy mouthful of pineapple. "A witch can't change time. That's one of the rules."

"You're kidding," said Sabrina. The bus was due any second.

"Nope."

"Gotta go!" Sabrina snatched up her backpack and was out the door in a flash.

"You also can't get rid of cellulite!" Hilda yelled after her.

All through the bus ride, Sabrina kept sneaking peeks at her fellow students. Were any of them staring at her differently than they had the day before? Could they sense a change in her? Was the word "witch" written across her forehead for all to see?

Westbridge High School was just as chaotic and intimidating the second morning as it had been on the first. The same crowds of jostling teenagers in the halls, the same strangeness to the surroundings, the same sense that Sabrina somehow didn't belong.

But then Jenny sailed up behind her, and Sabrina realized that at least one person was happy to see her.

"Got a joke," said Jenny. "Knock-knock."

Sabrina was willing to bite. "Who's there?"

"Brad."

"Brad who?"

"Brad Pitt," Jenny said smugly. "Is there any other Brad worth mentioning?" Both girls laughed as they headed for their first class.

That joke was the high point of the day, Sabrina decided later. Or maybe the day was just cursed from the start.

It was only the second day of school, but Mrs. Hecht, the history teacher, decided to find out how much her students knew about the subject. A black woman with the tidy cornrows, she was a perfect sweetheart as a human being, but as an examiner she could have given lessons to Torquemada and the Spanish Inquisition. Fifty minutes and a hundred numbered questions later, Sabrina and Jenny staggered out to the hallway.

"Thank you all for coming," chirped Mrs. Hecht. "Did you enjoy that pop quiz?"

"I am *so* bad at history," Jenny complained.

"Me too," agreed Sabrina. "I mean, how are we supposed to remember things that happened so long ago?"

Before Jenny could answer, a football came flying down the hall, narrowly missing several students in the crowd. "Heads up!" somebody shouted.

The warning came too late. The football hit Sabrina's forehead and bounced off. "Ow!" she yelped.

Jenny shouted at the unseen thrower. "Hey! Watch it with the football!" She turned back to Sabrina. "Are you okay?"

Sabrina was too mortified to speak. Everyone had seen her get bonked. She felt even lower when she realized that Libby and her crew had been walking behind her all the time. The brunette cheerleader shouldered past Sabrina, sneering, "Try to live in this world, not just your own. *Freak.*"

"Witch" might not have been written on Sabrina's forehead, but "Freak" might as well have been. She resisted the temptation to see if her back bore a Kick Me sign.

Events continued with the same awkwardness until lunch. She and Jenny found seats in the small cafeteria and tried to relax. Looking around the room, Sabrina realized that she had overlooked something about the place the day before. The walls were painted a pale gray with wide blue and gold horizontal stripes that circled the room— standard industrial-design blandness. But on the long wall opposite the steam tables was a painted logo of the school mascot, an angry-looking vegetable running through the school team name.

"The football team's name is the Fighting Scallions?" Sabrina asked Jenny in disbelief.

Jenny giggled. "Well, it was supposed to be the

Fighting *Stallions,* but the printer made a typo. And since he was donating his services, nobody had the heart to correct the mistake."

Sabrina stared at the cartoon scallion and laughed. "Sure gives a new twist to the term 'rooting for the home team!'"

"Ahem . . . Can I sit here?" The voice was male and friendly. It belonged to the hunk that Libby had stolen and monopolized during biology class. He loomed over the table, smiling his shy smile and gripping a tray piled high with food. He wore an oversize sweatshirt over a dark shirt and jeans. On his muscular frame, the clothes looked loose, not baggy.

Sabrina couldn't help but grin at this unexpected stroke of good luck. "Sure," she said. Jenny shot her a look of suppressed excitement. Having Harvey sit with them would be a *major* coup.

Harvey settled himself, then looked at Sabrina with concern in his eyes. "How's your head?" he asked.

"It kinda hurts." *Oh, no,* thought Sabrina, *he saw me get hit?* She resisted the urge to slide under the table.

A guilty look crossed Harvey's handsome features. "Sorry," he said hesitantly. "You know I didn't *mean* to hit you with the football."

"Oh. That was you?" Sabrina suddenly brightened. Harvey nodded sheepishly. "You have a really good arm."

"Thanks. I'm trying out for the team, but the

coach thinks I need to put on twenty pounds." He pointed apologetically at the pile of food on his plate.

Sabrina groped for a way to prolong the conversation. "Do you know Jenny?"

Harvey studied the girl with the forest of long red curls. "You live in the house with the funny mailbox, right?"

Jenny blushed with embarrassment. "It's not our fault," she said by way of explanation. "The people who lived there before us were actually named Mr. and Mrs. Hogg."

"Nah, it's cute," Harvey said, smiling broadly. "My mailbox is boring. It's really just a place to put letters." He looked thoughtful and confused at the same time, as if his mailbox should be offering him something more but he hadn't an idea of what.

"Mine, too!" bubbled Sabrina, a little too enthusiastically.

Then Sabrina's brief moment of happiness was darkened by the shadow of doom—Libby, carrying her lunch tray to the trash basket. The cheerleader stopped behind Sabrina, pointedly ignoring her, and batted her mascaraed eyelashes at Harvey. "Hi, Harvey," she cooed. "I'm having a party on Saturday night. You'll be there, right?"

Harvey paused as if he hadn't the slightest idea how to reply. Then he shrugged amiably and said, "Sure. I'm not doing anything else."

"Perfect. Everyone cool's coming," Libby gloated. There was a moment of silence. Then and only then did Libby look down at Sabrina. "Well, that's all."

Once again Libby had snatched Harvey out from under Sabrina's nose. And this time there was no question of her action not being deliberate. Sabrina turned to glare at the smug cheerleader.

Libby started to move away, tilting her tray as she spun. A half-full glass of grape soda spilled over Sabrina's arm and down the front of her print blouse. "Oh, no," Libby said in mock horror. Then she flashed a wicked grin. "Smell you later," she chirped over her shoulder as she left.

Sabrina stood up angrily. "You did that on purpose!" she shouted.

Without turning around, Libby said dismissively, "Prove it!"

A hot rush of anger made Sabrina tremble. She bolted to her feet and yelled, "Don't walk away!" Libby ignored her and kept going. "I mean it!" Sabrina yelled, jabbing an accusing finger at the cheerleader's back. "I'm not done talking with you . . . you . . . you—" Her voice seemed to echo, bouncing from wall to wall like the wailing of a tormented ghost.

The cafeteria suddenly darkened, and the temperature dropped a dozen degrees. An unexpected clap of thunder rattled glasses and silverware on the tables, and a wild wind whipped through the room, scattering napkins and unraveling hairdos. The students of Westbridge High squealed in alarm and dived for cover.

"Windstorm!" someone shouted, despite the fact that New England rarely had windstorms—and never inside a building. "Everybody hit the dirt!"

Sabrina stood frozen in position, rooted to the spot by a combination of terror and distant fascination. Her whole body quivered as energy crackled and surged through her, looking for a pathway out. Suddenly a bright spark leaped from her finger and flashed across the room toward Libby. In an electric instant the obnoxious cheerleader disappeared.

The room grew silent. Students peeped up over tables and chairs to see what was left of the room. Sabrina didn't even notice them. Her arm dropped to her side of its own accord. She couldn't seem to move anything else. Teenagers started milling about as she stood dumbstruck in the center of the cafeteria.

"Wh-where did Libby go?" Jenny asked in confusion as she and Harvey rose from behind their table.

Sabrina struggled for control. "I have no idea," she barely managed to stammer.

Then she ran toward the door, slowing only to scoop up the pineapple that sat in the very spot where Libby had last stood.

☆

# Chapter 4

☆

Zelda sat at the kitchen table, reading the latest issue of the *Journal of American Theoretical Physicists* while Hilda took a pineapple upside-down cake from the oven and set it next to three others to cool.

"Oh, goody, there's a lecture at M.I.T. on the Heisenberg uncertainty principle," said Zelda. Then her brow creased as she read the fine print. "It's either at eight o'clock or at ten."

Hilda didn't have a chance to comment, because just then Sabrina stormed in from the porch carrying the Libby-pineapple. "I *hate* being a witch!" she yelled, thrusting the pineapple out at her aunts, "I just turned the most popular girl in school into a pineapple!"

"Why?" asked Hilda, as if this sort of thing happened every day. Given Hilda's impulsive nature, perhaps it did.

"It's the only thing you taught me how to do!" cried Sabrina in tearful exasperation.

"Chill," said Hilda, taking the pineapple from her niece's hands. "I can fix this."

She took the fruit over to the butcher-block table and slid a big cleaver out of its rack. She poised the blade over the pineapple and asked, "Chunks or rings?"

"Hilda," Zelda warned her sister, "there are other ways."

"Wedges?" replied Hilda in honest confusion.

"Sabrina doesn't know how to seal her spells yet, so . . ." Zelda moved both hands in an intricate pattern. "The popular girl is not a fruit!" she intoned. Sparks leaped from her fingers and zapped the pineapple. It shimmered and began changing shape. An instant later Libby lay curled up on the butcher block. "There. All better," Zelda pronounced.

Libby's eyes fell on Sabrina and then took in the rest of the Spellman kitchen. With a quaver in her voice, she demanded, "What am I doing in your house?"

Sabrina blurted out the first thing that came to mind. "You . . . came over for a visit?" she ventured.

Libby's confusion shifted to snobbish scorn. Whatever mystery surrounded her presence here, on this topic she knew where she stood. "I did not!" she insisted. She slid down from the block and started backing out of the room, flinching when she saw Sabrina's aunts. She might not have known how she got there, but she automatically tried to assume control of the situation. "You did something to me," she accused Sabrina. "You sent me . . . somewhere. It was small and it smelled like Hawaii!"

"Look, Libby, I'm sorry—" Sabrina began.

"Not as sorry as you *will* be," snapped Libby in a rising fury. She was frightened, and she struck back using the weapon she knew best—intimidation. "You're an even *bigger* freak than I thought. And the whole school's going to know it!" She bolted through the French doors and disappeared—under her own power this time, not magically.

Sabrina was dumbstruck. Hilda, however, jumped right in to defend her original solution to the problem. "See?" she said, pointing at the departing Libby. "My way, she'd be on a tooth-pick."

The full weight of the cursed day dropped on Sabrina like a mountain. The upheaval of her life, her eccentric aunts, her social doom—it wasn't fair! "It's over," she moaned, crumpling into a chair. "My life is over. I mean, it's not just over, but *over* over!"

Zelda put a reassuring hand on her niece's shoulder. "Oh, stop, Sabrina. Libby can't hurt you. She's just one person with a crazy story. No one will believe her."

"She's a cheerleader," Sabrina whined. "Nobody has more credibility. The only way to make this better is to turn back time, and you said a witch can't do that."

A moment of profound silence passed before Zelda said slowly, *"A* witch can't. But *collectively* we have powers that a single witch doesn't." She groped for a suitable explanation. "It's a union thing."

Sabrina felt a flicker of hope. "So it's possible?"

"You can appeal to the Witches' Council," Zelda said. Then she hurriedly added, "But they grant time-reversal requests only in *extreme* cases."

"Like for two months a bunny ruled all of England," stuck in Hilda.

"When?" asked Sabrina, confused. Granted, she had failed her history quiz, but she knew she would have remembered something *that* weird.

"See?" Hilda shot back smugly. "It wasn't until he traded India for a head of lettuce that the council decided to erase him."

Sabrina clung to the thread of hope. "How do I get to this Witches' Council?"

"It's ten million light-years away," explained Zelda.

Sabrina's face fell. This magic stuff seemed to move with a one-step-forward, two-steps-back kind of progress. You could do anything—except this, that, that, and—oh, yes—this other thing. It seemed there was an exception to every rule. What if there were more exceptions than rules?

Sabrina's sudden silence bothered Zelda. Then she recalled something she hadn't yet told her niece. "But . . . there's a shortcut through our linen closet."

Having more exceptions than rules might be a good thing.

Moments later Zelda and Hilda led Sabrina up the back stairs to the closet opposite her bedroom. Zelda maintained a machine-gun commentary all the way up the stairs, trying to fill Sabrina in as quickly as possible. "The head of the Witches' Council is named Drell. He's a mean, pigheaded, power-mad despot."

"We used to date," Hilda admitted, as if confessing to a lapse in taste. "Haven't seen him in centuries."

"Not since he left her at the altar," Zelda elaborated. "Daddy lost a *huge* deposit on the Parthenon."

Hilda glared at her older sister. "Would you let that go? It's ancient history."

This was obviously an old argument, and Zelda wasn't about to drop the topic that easily. "*I* knew Drell was bad news . . ." she lectured.

"I mean, I didn't even *want* the big wedding . . ." Hilda insisted.

". . . but you wanted to be his ninety-third wife."

". . . with the long white toga—"

"Excuse me," interrupted Sabrina. "I'm trying to turn back time here. Can we go?" She opened the door to the linen closet and gestured for her aunts to lead the way.

Hilda blanched and drew back. "Oh, no. I couldn't. I swore I would never speak to Drell again as long as he lived."

"Besides, Sabrina, the council will respect you more if you go alone," said Zelda. She pointed into the depths of the closet. "Make a left at the towels and follow the signs."

Feeling a little ridiculous, Sabrina walked into the closet, the spicy sting of laundry soap and fabric softener making her nose wrinkle. Her aunts continued to call advice after her.

"Watch out for Drell!" warned Hilda.

"And whatever you do, don't stare at his mole!" shouted Zelda.

The door shut behind Sabrina, leaving her alone. She stared at the sheets and towels stacked neatly on shelves at the back of the closet. *This* was a path that jumped ten million light-years? Were her aunts playing some sort of joke on her? But then she remembered Libby-the-pineapple and the doom that awaited her at school tomorrow. She took a deep breath and plunged ahead. But she put her hands out—just in case the wall was really there.

It wasn't. Instead, there was a blinding flash of light and a tooth-rattling rumble. Then there was a sense of rushing, even though she was standing still. Although she was just a novice at magic, Sabrina could feel the webs of energy around her, channeling vast forces to punch holes in space and time. The sensation made her skin tingle.

Then, without warning, Sabrina found herself stumbling forward through a different linen closet. Her hands hit the door and knocked it open. She caught her balance outside the closet, just as the door slammed shut behind her. Feeling something in her hand, Sabrina discovered that somewhere during her trip she'd picked up a washcloth. A pink one.

The place that the Witches' Council called home looked like nothing Sabrina had ever seen before. All around her was a vast blue space flecked with clouds, as if she were high up in the sky. A wide patterned carpet stretched from the linen closet to a long table made of a dark wood.

Sabrina stared for a moment at the carpet. The lines in its pattern seemed to writhe and pulse to a slow rhythm. In fact, they appeared to be more like roots than lines. Then she saw that the legs of the table actually sprouted out of the carpet like ancient oak trees. Vines and creepers grew up from the carpet as well, forming a verdant tablecloth embellished with leaves. A massive marble pillar hovered in midair behind the table, serving as a pedestal for an immense green apple.

A single candle in a silver holder threw flickering light over the stacks of parchment and paper that covered the table. It also illuminated the three oddly dressed individuals who sat talking behind the table.

"Listen, people, Cher keeps calling me about finding another Oscar-winning role. Can someone else handle this?" That was the man at the center of the table, who was examining a slip of pink parchment with writing on it. He was the largest man Sabrina had ever seen; she thought maybe he was a small giant. He wore a floral brocade dressing gown over a fancy shirt with enormous lace sleeves and a neckcloth pinned with a huge amber brooch. His hair was even curlier than Jenny's, and he peered at papers through round, black-rimmed glasses. In his left hand he held a large brown mole, which he absently petted and stroked with his other hand when he wasn't shuffling paper.

To his left sat an elfin man dressed in a dark suit and a bowler that was probably all the rage in England—about fifty years before Sabrina was born. He nodded and grinned impishly at the large man but uttered no sound.

At the end of the table closest to Sabrina sat a regal woman with curly blond hair piled high on her head. She wore a black overdress with a flared collar that rose higher than her head and framed her face, accentuating her pale skin, ruby lips, and darting eyes. Of the three, she bore the closest resemblance to a traditional witch, if that witch was also an Elizabethan court lady.

Sabrina felt the urge to shrink as they all turned to look at her. "Is—is this the Witches' Council?" she stammered.

"Yes. I don't believe you have an appointment,"

the blond woman said. She bent forward to examine a large volume in front of her. The candle flickered, its waxy body bending and quivering, making the woman squint. "No, you're not in the book. Drell, did you remember to feed the candle?"

The big man in the middle looked annoyed. He raised the slip of parchment with Cher's request on it and touched it to the candle flame. There was a bright flash, and the candle brightened and stood up straight. "There," Drell said in a grumpy tone. "Happy, Cassandra?"

Sabrina wondered if all witches were distracted by petty occurrences. She tried to take charge of the conversation. "I know I don't have an appointment, but"—she groped for a conclusion—"brought a washcloth?"

This seemed to please the pixieish man at the end. He snapped his fingers at Sabrina, motioning for her to hand him the washcloth. When she gave it to him, he immediately took a bite out of it and began to chew with gusto.

Drell glared at him. "Next time, Skippy, hold out for a hand towel," he snapped. Then he gruffly addressed Sabrina. "State your name, age, and request. We'll see if we can fit you in."

"I'm Sabrina, I'm sixteen, and I'd like to turn back time."

*"Denied!* Ha-ha-ha-hee!" Drell rumbled with sarcastic laughter. "Well, we did fit you in. Next order of business?" He dismissed Sabrina with a wave of a beringed hand. When she didn't move, Drell's

expression darkened. "Are you staring at my mole?" he growled suspiciously.

"N-no!" said Sabrina. "I just haven't had a chance to explain *why* I want to turn back time."

Cassandra, who had been looking terminally bored, perked up at this. "Let's humor her," she said.

Drell shrugged. "Okay. Speak! But quickly."

"Where do I start?" said Sabrina, half to herself. 'Well, from the moment I arrived at my new school, I didn't fit in. I wore the wrong shoes—which may seem like nothing, but kids can be *so* judgmental—"

"I said quickly!" Drell snapped. He spiraled his hand at Sabrina in a hurry-up gesture.

Sabrina suddenly began talking like a tape played at double speed. "SobythetimeIgottothecafeteria andLibbyspilledgrapejuiceonme,Iwasalreadyabit tense. That'swhyIturnedherintoapineapple.Imean, itwasn'tmyfault.Youdon'tknowthisgirl.She'snota witchbutshehasthepowertoturnthewholeschool againstme.Andfrankly—"

Drell's hand stopped, and Sabrina's voice returned to normal. "I never asked to be a witch, and life is hard enough knowing you really *are* a freak without everyone else knowing it, too."

Drell rubbed noses with his mole. "Oh, the problems of teenagers are *so* interesting," he crooned to it. The little rodent just stared back at him, unmoving. In fact, Sabrina couldn't recall having seen the mole move at all. Was it alive? Was it a stuffed mole? She tore her eyes away as Drell lifted his head. It wouldn't be good for her to get caught staring at his mole.

"We will review your case and get back to you," Drell said dismissively.

"But I need to know—" Sabrina began.

"And you *will,*" barked Drell. "Now go! And don't let the time-space continuum hit you on the way out."

Skippy looked up from his half-eaten washcloth to waggle his fingers in a good-bye wave.

Sabrina bolted for the closet door. Behind her she could hear Drell murmuring affectionately to his pet. "You love me, huh, don't you, Moley?" Then there was thunder and lightning, and she was home.

Late that night Sabrina lay brooding on her bed in her nightgown. The cat was snoring gently on the windowsill. "Psst, Salem, I can't sleep."

Salem yawned and licked his chops. "Then I guess there's no reason why *I* should."

Sabrina ignored his sarcasm. Cats were snotty by nature. "Do you think the Witches' Council will grant my time-reversal request?" she asked him.

"I'm the wrong witch to ask," said Salem. "They weren't very lenient with me. I was sentenced to a hundred years as a cat. And for what?"

"I don't know. For what?" Sabrina's interest was piqued.

"Oh, like any young kid, I dreamed of world

domination." Salem flexed his claws. "Of course, they really crack down when you act on it."

"Wow. No wonder you're so possessive of the sofa."

"Mmm." Salem's eyes narrowed as he reminisced. "It would have been glorious. Me as the firm but just emperor of earth." His tail twitched in annoyance. "Trust me, being a house pet wasn't even Plan B."

"Come on. Your life can't be that bad. You take five thousand naps a day."

"I can't go dancing. I can't play squash. The sound of the can opener is the only thing that makes me feel truly alive." He stared off into space. It was hard to tell, but he almost looked depressed.

"Salem," said Sabrina softly, "would you like me to bring you your rubber mouse?"

Salem tried mightily to maintain a proper feline dignity. That effort lasted about ten seconds. "Please," he said.

The morning sun found Sabrina floating over her bed. The alarm clock rang, and she automatically turned to slap it silent. The movement woke her up and with that, her levitation abruptly ceased. The drop to the bed knocked all the wind out of her.

There were definite disadvantages to floating in your sleep.

A short while later she sat in the kitchen, killing time with her aunt Zelda. Hilda came bounding down the stairs, her activity cutting through the gloom like a knife. "Any word from the Witches' Council?"

"Not yet," said Sabrina glumly. "And if I'm going to school, I'll have to leave any second."

A clunking noise echoed through the kitchen, and a white envelope popped up from the toaster.

"That's it!" exclaimed Zelda.

"That's it?" said Sabrina in disbelief. She plucked the envelope out of the toaster slot.

"Careful, don't burn your fingers."

"Please, please, please . . ." Sabrina chanted as she took the envelope and opened it. There was nothing inside—no note, no writing of any kind.

"Request denied!" Drell's voice boomed right out of the envelope. His scornful laughter echoed through the kitchen. *"Heh-heh-heh-heh!"*

Sabrina slumped down on the table. Zelda put her hand on her niece's. "I'm sorry, honey."

"It's okay," said Sabrina, sitting up again. Then she forced cheerfulness into her voice. "So . . . where are we moving? I hear Greenland's a groove."

Hilda took a sterner tack. "Get your books. You're going to be late."

"You don't understand, Aunt Hilda. I'm not going to school."

"Oh, yes, you are!" Hilda insisted. "You can do this. You can't go through life being afraid of things. Toughen up!"

"But everyone will laugh at me," Sabrina whined.

47

"Toughen up!" Hilda ordered again.

"So that's my choice? Toughen up . . . or toughen up?" Sabrina said in disbelief. "Aunt Zelda, will you help me?"

Zelda stood up next to her sister, the two of them presenting a united front to their niece. "You know I hate to say it, but your aunt Hilda is right." Hilda smiled smugly. "I mean, who cares what the other kids say?"

Sabrina sighed. "Actually, Libby thought I was a freak even before this happened."

"See?" her aunts said in unison.

"Fine. I surrender." Sabrina headed for the coatrack by the door to pick up her backpack. "I guess every school needs a weird kid. Might as well be me."

"I was the weird kid!" blurted Hilda, trying to be helpful. Sabrina shrugged and shuffled out the back way.

Zelda looked wistfully after her niece. "They don't tar and feather anymore, do they?" she asked softly. "I hated that."

Hilda thrust her jaw forward in irritation. "You know whose fault this is? Drell's. What a jerk. I can't believe I ever went out with him." She stalked over to the island and grabbed a loaf of bread from the bread box.

Zelda rolled her eyes and pursed her lips. "Just a thought, but I'll bet you could persuade him to change his mind," she prodded her sister.

"Me? I don't think so." Hilda put a couple of

slices in the toaster. "Besides, Sabrina's going to be fine. Yes, she'll be ostracized and reviled. But that's what high school is all about. The wounds will heal, the scars will fade. . . ." She screwed her face up in frustration. "You know I can't face Drell!"

Zelda stared down her nose at her sister. She crossed her arms and said firmly, "Toughen up."

Hilda hesitated for a moment, then squared her shoulders and marched up the stairs toward the linen closet. "It's payback time, Drell! I'm coming in!" She barreled into the closet and slammed the door behind her.

Lightning flashed and thunder rumbled inside the closet. Then Drell's surprised voice boomed out, "Hilda! What are you doing here? Whoa! Take your hands off my mole!"

# Chapter 5

Sabrina wished she'd looked up a spell for invisibility before coming to school. How could her life be over before she even began her third day at Westbridge High? As she weaved her way through the crowded halls before first period, she was convinced that everyone was staring at her, thinking, There goes the freak witch! She half expected a welcoming committee armed with torches and wooden Frankenstein rakes.

She was so wound up that she jumped when Jenny appeared behind her. "Got a joke," said Jenny. "Knock-knock."

Starting the day with a lame joke seemed better than being chased by a mob of peasants—er, students—so Sabrina bit. "Who's there?" she replied glumly.

"Brad." Jenny grinned.

Not only a lame joke but a rerun. Sabrina stepped on Jenny's punch line. "Brad Pitt," she said quickly. "You told me that joke yesterday."

Jenny gave Sabrina a strange look. "N-no I didn't," she said slowly. "I just heard it on the bus." Then she shrugged and sped on down the hall.

"Really . . ." Sabrina murmured to herself. Did she dare to let herself hope?

Her spirits soared when she walked into history class and Mrs. Hecht announced a pop quiz. Suddenly the day became brighter.

"Excellent work, Sabrina!" Mrs. Hecht bubbled as the students left her classroom.

"I can't believe you aced that pop quiz!" Jenny said in amazement as they hit the halls.

"Hey, what can I say?" Sabrina said smugly. "I just love history." Then she spun around, looking for the football that she knew was heading straight for her head. Out of the corner of her eye she saw Libby walking nearby.

"Heads up!" Harvey yelled from down the hall. Sabrina caught the football in midair.

"Great catch!" called someone in the crowd. Sabrina bobbed her head to acknowledge the compliment. Libby just stared frosty daggers at Sabrina as the haughty cheerleader brushed by. Sabrina smiled to herself and started plotting how the rest of the day *should* go.

By the time Harvey asked, "Can I sit here?" at the lunch table with her and Jenny, Sabrina felt a confidence and strength she thought she'd never feel again.

"Sure," she replied, smiling her warmest smile at him.

"That was a great catch," Harvey said as he sat down.

"I was in the zone," Sabrina said modestly. This felt like going through the steps of a dance. "Do you know Jenny?"

Harvey looked at the redheaded girl. "You live in the house with the funny mailbox, right?" he began.

It was time for Sabrina to lead. She interrupted before Jenny could answer. "Before we get into that . . . if you're not doing anything Saturday night, want to come see a movie with Jenny and me?"

Harvey seemed startled by such an idea. Then he nodded, "Sure. That sounds like fun." He grinned. "Cool."

"Cool," agreed Sabrina.

"Cool," said Jenny, admiring how Sabrina had reserved some time with such a cute guy so quickly.

Sabrina felt pleased beyond belief. "Now, you were saying about mailboxes . . .?"

Right on schedule, Libby sailed by with her tray and her glass of grape soda. "Hi, Harvey," she cooed. "I'm having a party Saturday night. You'll be there, right?"

Harvey's gaze darted from Libby to Sabrina and back again. "Sorry. I just made plans."

Libby's jaw dropped.

Amused, Sabrina wondered if anyone had ever said no to the cheerleader before. She couldn't resist rubbing it in. "Ooh. Bubble-burst," she said, mock sympathy dripping from her lips. "And I'll bet you wanted everyone cool to come."

Libby's lip curled into a resentful sneer, and her tray tilted forward. Sabrina flicked a finger, and the toppling cup of grape soda spun about and spilled the purple liquid *upward,* splattering Libby's face.

Libby shrieked in shock and fury and raced out of the cafeteria. Sabrina and her friends collapsed in laughter.

Sabrina burst into the kitchen bubbling over with happiness. Zelda and Hilda were sitting at the table with bowls of pineapple chunks on toothpicks in front of them.

"I *love* being a witch!" shrieked Sabrina. "I don't know what made the councillors change their minds, but I got to live the whole day over!" She danced around the room, bouncing her way toward the stairs. "Now the teachers think I'm smart, the jocks think I'm cool—oh, and I'm going to the movies with Harvey and Jenny on Saturday night! Yahoo! I'm normal!" She paused at the bottom of the stairs. "Gotta go tell the cat!" She raced up to her room.

"Teens . . ." said Hilda wistfully.

Zelda smiled. "What about them?"

"Just in general . . ."

Zelda patted her younger sister's arm. "That was very brave of you. You should tell Sabrina what you did."

"Oh, no! It was an act of total selflessness. I just wanted to help my niece. And I helped myself a little, too."

"You did? How?"

Hilda nearly levitated off the chair. She almost looked like a giddy teenager herself. "Drell and I have a date on Saturday night!" she announced gleefully.

Zelda was horrified. "Oh, no, not again! He left you at the altar!"

"He had a good excuse."

"He had three hundred years to think it up!"

"Would you give him another second chance?"

"How many centuries do you need to learn this guy's a jerk?"

"You never *could* get past the mole. . . ."

Sabrina could hear her aunts bickering downstairs, but she tuned them out. She lifted the black cat up from his sunny spot by the window. "Salem," she said, "I don't play squash, but how 'bout a dance?" She held the cat up, her hands just under his front legs, and swung him around in time to imaginary music. Salem, like a true cat, tried to pretend it wasn't happening.

# Chapter 6

☆

With her life saved from total disaster by sorcerous time reversal, Sabrina settled into the routine of life in a new town and a new school. The first few weeks sped by, each seeming to bring its own little adventure. Each day Sabrina tried to navigate her way through the treacherous waters of learning and teenage social politics, just like everyone else. Each night, however, she studied the great leather-bound book of magic, trying to come to terms with her secret life as a witch.

Eventually, her ability to cast small spells and shift reality around to obey her will acquired a sort of familiarity, if not normalcy. The most obvious improvement in her life was the tidiness of her room—she still changed her outfit a dozen times before deciding what to wear, but magical dressing meant no piles of not-quite-rights on the floor.

Even so, learning to *think* like a witch didn't come naturally. Sometimes it was hard to remember that there could be a magical solution to a problem—like the ice-cream incident.

Sabrina had come home from school one day to find her aunts sitting like statues at the kitchen table. She immediately started to worry. Had some spell gone wrong and left them immobilized? Had some sorcerous prankster frozen them in their tracks?

Closer examination revealed that the Spellman sisters were staring with total concentration on an enormous jigsaw puzzle laid out on the table. The rim of the puzzle was complete, hinting at a scene that was mostly turbulent clouds and sky. Without looking up, Zelda suddenly said, "I need a piece of sky with a smidge of smoke and a slightly bulbous doohickey."

Hilda's head didn't budge from her scrutiny, but her hand snatched up a small piece and thrust it at her sister. "Here you go," she offered.

"Thanks." Zelda accepted the piece and pushed it into place without otherwise moving.

"It's funny," Hilda muttered as her eyes scanned the pile for matching pieces, "but when you live a thousand years, jigsaw puzzles don't seem like such a waste of time."

*Great,* thought Sabrina. *This is what I have to look forward to?* She sailed into the kitchen, calling brightly, "I'm home!"

Neither of her aunts looked up from the puzzle. Hilda did greet her, however. "Hi, Sabrina. How was school?"

"Great. Libby dropped her lunch tray for the third day in a row." Sabrina grinned mischievously. "I'm getting really good at that."

Zelda put another piece into place, finishing an image of a large balloon. She stood up and crowed, "Yes! Now you can read *'Hindenberg!'*"

Sabrina was halfway to the refrigerator. She shot a puzzled glance at her elder aunt and then shook her head. She moved on to open the door to the freezer compartment. "Darn!" she groused. "We're all out of ice cream."

The mention of food got her younger aunt's attention. Hilda looked up from the table and regarded her niece critically. "Haven't you forgotten something?"

"I know, I shouldn't eat before dinner." *Adults,* thought Sabrina.

"No. We're witches." Hilda made a gesture at the freezer that was halfway between a shiver and a scooping motion. When Sabrina looked in again, she saw a half-dozen pints of ice cream stacked neatly in front of the frozen vegetables. "Dig in."

"Cool." *Adult witches,* Sabrina corrected herself.

Back to looking for the *Hindenberg*'s left rear propeller, Zelda intoned, "And you *shouldn't* eat before dinner!"

Sabrina disappeared up the stairs with a pint.

Aunt Zelda was a witch, yes, but she was always an adult first.

The next morning found Sabrina perched on the pink settee at the foot of her bed, flipping frantically through her magic book. Salem lay sleeping on the blue bedspread, a slight frosting of white on his whiskers and ears showing that he had cleaned out the last of the ice cream from the empty pint container in the wastebasket.

Magic had shortened the time it took for Sabrina to dress for school, but she was discovering that there were definite limits to what sorcery could accomplish. Without making her late for school, of course.

"Rollerblades . . . Why can't I find a spell for Rollerblades? Salem, help me," she said, appealing to the cat. "It's like you don't care."

Salem yawned and opened one eye. "Oh, I care. I care deeply about your . . . what was it?"

"Rollerblades," Sabrina repeated, thumping the open page. "But they're not in the *R*'s."

Salem had found the sweet residue on his whiskers and was dabbing at them with a freshly licked paw. "Did you check under Sporting Goods?" he prompted.

Sabrina flipped pages excitedly. "Let's see . . ." Something caught her eye. "Here's 'Sporting *Events*—to win, lose, or tie.' Huh, that's all you have to do to influence the game?" She pumped her fist vertically twice and then pointed. "Easier than you'd think."

"Hey, don't mess around with that spell," Salem warned, "unless you give me time to call my bookie first."

"Here it is, 'Sporting Goods.' And they've got in-line skates."

"Great!" Salem yawned. "Can I go back to sleep now?"

"Sure," Sabrina said absently as she studied the spell.

She repeated the instructions to herself twice, then looked around her room for supplies. "Okay, I need an old shoe box." She dived to the floor and fished around under her bed. A second later a dusty but serviceable Lady Footgear box sat on the settee. "And for speed, I need a gift from a quick-footed animal." Sabrina reached over and plucked a few hairs from Salem's tail.

"Ow! That wasn't a *gift*," the cat complained.

Sabrina put the hairs into the shoebox and replaced the lid. She stood up and pointed her finger at the box. "Here goes. Come on, Roller-blades."

The shoebox shimmered, then shifted shape, becoming wider, broader, deeper. The pale blue stripes skittered around on the cardboard, fragmenting to become letters and pictures. A moment later the shoebox had become a gaudy package.

"Yes, it worked!" Sabrina exulted. "Excellent! I

made"—she read the package label closely—"Rollerblahs?"

Hilda came breezing into the bedroom. Being a natural morning person, she was already dressed for the day in a tight denim vest over a black long-sleeved knitted top. To soften the effect, she wore a flouncy skirt in a large pastel flower print. For a change, she was concerned about someone else's appetite. "Sabrina, you want some breakfast?"

Sabrina was dejected by her failure with the skates. "No, thanks. I'll be out Rollerblahing."

Hilda was never one to let someone else's problem lie. "What's wrong?" she asked.

Salem looked up from his licking—what had started as a quick touch-up had progressed into a full-scale bath. "She wanted in-line skates, but she asked for a brand name."

"Oh, you can't do that. We've had strict copyright laws ever since the seventies when witches *way* overdid Gucci."

"You can still get decent knockoffs from the Hong Kong witches," added Salem. Of course, Salem would know how to bend the rules, whatever they were.

Sabrina was inconsolable. "I don't care about labels. I just care about quality. Rollerblahs aren't the same. I mean, even the kid on the box isn't having fun." She pointed to the illustration, which showed a miserable teenage boy with his arm in a blue nylon sling.

"Well, since you've got your heart set on a brand

name, there's only one thing to do," Hilda said, putting an arm around Sabrina confidentially.

"You'll buy me real Rollerblades?" squealed Sabrina.

"No," snapped her aunt. "You can get a job like the rest of us."

Sabrina pouted, but quick as lightning, Hilda tickled her ribs until the teenager collapsed to the floor in helpless laughter.

# Chapter 7

Later that morning Sabrina stood in front of the Wall of Doom, as the students called the job postings outside the guidance office. Faithful Jenny stood at her side, offering comments and advice.

Sabrina read from a faded index card at the top left corner of the bulletin board. "'Baby-sitter needed—triplets.'"

"That card's been up there for years," Jenny warned.

Sabrina despaired. Working for what you wanted seemed like a miserable way to spend a life. She turned to her friend. "How about where you work? Do they need anybody else at the stables?"

"We always need people to shovel," Jenny said helpfully. "You gag a lot, but most people never throw up."

Sabrina smiled politely. "Maybe I should keep

looking." Her eyes scanned the board again. "Wow. 'Earn money watching TV.'" A hand darted forward and snatched the posting away. Sabrina turned just in time to see the back of a girl as she raced away. "Hey, that was mine!" she shouted at the retreating figure.

A sarcastic voice floated back, "You've got to be more aggressive in this job market!"

"It's just as well," Jenny consoled her friend. "Watching TV is too pure an experience to taint with money."

"True," agreed Sabrina. Her eyes moved across the board again. "Here's another baby-sitting job. And they have just one kid."

"Go for it," urged Jenny.

A hand moved into Sabrina's range of vision, reaching for the slip of paper pinned to the cork. Her own hand flashed out and ripped the paper off the pushpin. She glared at the girl who'd tried to beat her out of the job, then headed for the phone bank.

Sabrina stood in front of one of the phones by Principal LaRue's office. The class bell had rung, but she was determined to nail down this baby-sitting job. She spoke quickly to Mrs. Gerson, the woman who had posted the note. "I have references, and I really love children. In fact, I even was one."

"Tonight! Can you start tonight?" The voice on

the phone sounded harried, and the woman kept being interrupted by what sounded like a tag-team match with her unseen son.

"Tonight? Really?" Sabrina hadn't thought of starting work that soon, but this wasn't an opportunity to miss.

"Rudy! Don't eat the plant!" Mrs. Gerson sounded exhausted. "Yes, tonight."

"Okay. Great."

"Thank you." Mrs. Gerson sounded pathetically relieved. "My husband and I never get out, and there are only so many videos you can rent—"

"I really should go to class," Sabrina interrupted as politely as she could.

Mrs. Gerson's voice rose an octave. "No, please don't hang up! I need adult conversation! What's happening in the world?"

"Look, I'll see you tonight, and in the meantime you can watch *MTV News.*" Sabrina set the receiver back on its hook as gently as she could and then raced off to biology class.

She slid the classroom door open quietly and tiptoed to her place at a lab table. Mr. Pool had his back to the class and was writing the word "Mitosis" on the blackboard. He greeted Sabrina without turning around. "Hi, Miss Spellman."

She flinched. "Hi, Mr. Pool," she answered mousily.

"I assume you have a weak, rambling, completely unacceptable excuse for being late."

"Well, see, I was—"

The lanky teacher turned to flash a sarcastic smile at her. "Never mind. I just remembered, I really prefer the sound of my own voice." He placed the chalk back in the tray with a precise and fussy flourish. "Tonight is Parents' Night, and I'm pretty darned excited. Why? I get to see which of you are the result of normal evolution and which are mutations that will be weeded out in the next generation." A forest of blank faces stared back at him, not reacting. "Oh, right, you all tanked the genetics unit."

He stared at his students like Sisyphus glaring at his rock after a coffee break. "Listen closely. I'm only going to say this once." He picked up the chalk again and began writing on the board at top speed: "Mitosis is the indirect method of nuclear division of cells, consisting of anaphase, metaphase, prophase . . ."

Pencils and pens flew over paper for the next forty-five minutes as Mr. Pool demonstrated an amazing ability to rattle off complex sentences with hardly a pause for breath. The end-of-class bell found him still shooting out facts in machine-gun delivery: ". . . leading to production of gametes in animals and spores in plants. And there you have it in a zygote."

He punctuated his last statement with a stab of chalk at the blackboard. The chalk shattered upon impact, speckling Mr. Pool's frayed sleeve with white dust. He grimaced and stalked over to his desk, slapping at his arm. The students rose to hurry out of the classroom, but he had one last barb to toss at them. "All right," he yelled over the bustle. "Since we were able to cover so much material today, I'm going to move the test to tomorrow. Have fun studying tonight!"

Harvey frowned with uncharacteristic annoyance. "But, Mr. Pool, tonight's game four of the World Series."

Mr. Pool's voice dripped sarcasm. "No, really? Well, since I'll be stuck here with your parents, I guess we'll all miss the World Series together." He grinned evilly at the teenage boy. "Vindictive? Yes, but that's what gets me through the day."

Harvey caught up with Sabrina just outside the classroom. "Hey, Sabrina," he called, "my hand kinda cramped after 'mitosis is.' So I was wondering if we could get together and study tonight."

A slow flush crept over Sabrina's cheeks. She stared shyly at Harvey. "You and me?"

"Isn't that what 'we' means?" Harvey laughed.

"Yeah, sure." Sabrina's heart skipped a beat, but then her memory kicked in. "Oh, no! I can't. I'm baby-sitting tonight. But I'll bet you could come over. They're desperate."

"So it's cool?"

"Cool." As Harvey walked away, Sabrina pumped her fist in a triumphant *yes!*

* * *

Zelda took her coat from the rack by the French doors and called up to her sister, "Hilda, hurry up! We've got to go!" She put the coat down on a stool next to her purse and straightened the skirt of her powder-blue suit.

Salem sat near the sink on the island watching water drip from the faucet. "I still don't understand why I can't go to Parents' Night with you." He swiped at a drop, nearly hitting it.

"Because, Salem, it's weird enough that we're two sisters who live together in an old Victorian house," Zelda explained patiently. "If we show up with a cat, we cross the line into Looneyville."

Hilda came moping down the stairs, tugging at her long cream-colored jacket. "Zelda," she whined, "feel my head. I think I have a fever. I can't go to school."

"It's just Parents' Night."

"But I hate school," moaned Hilda, throwing herself into a chair. She was dressed as an adult, but her body language screamed "eight-year-old." A cranky eight-year-old. "Ohh, my stomach hurts!" She clutched her belly.

"Oh, grow up," her sister ordered. She pointed a cautionary finger. "And don't try making it snow."

Sabrina burst down the stairs and into the kitchen, then made a beeline for the doors to marvel at the weather. "Hey, it just started snowing. And it's really coming down!"

Zelda glared at her sister. "Hilda . . ."

The younger witch screwed up her face in protest but waggled her fingers at the door. "It stopped," she said petulantly. "There. No one was hurt."

A sudden screech of tires on ice snapped all three heads toward the doors. The screech ended with the sound of metal crumpling. Hilda flinched and ducked her head.

"I'm off to my baby-sitting job," announced Sabrina.

Zelda raked her eyes over the tight black top that Sabrina wore over black slacks and a white turtleneck. "You're all dressed up," she said knowingly.

"Well, I want to make a good impression on the baby." Sabrina flushed slightly under her perfect makeup. "And Harvey's going to be there."

"Ohhh," her aunts said in unison.

"Don't 'ohhh.' It's just a study date," Sabrina insisted.

"Uh-huh," they repeated.

"Don't 'uh-huh.' We have a test tomorrow."

"Mmm-hmm," purred Salem archly.

Sabrina glared at the cat. "Don't *you* start!" She turned back to her aunts. "Look, it's no big deal. Harvey could have asked anyone to study with him. Of course," she said smugly, "he did ask me. Gotta go."

Hilda watched her niece sail out the door. She hunted for another reason to delay her own departure. "You got any big plans for tonight, Salem?"

Salem fixed her with a feline's flat, dismissive gaze. "As soon as you leave, I'm going to listen to *Cats* and laugh myself silly."

Hilda's view was suddenly blocked by Zelda dangling a coat in front of her. Hilda snarled in helpless frustration.

# Chapter 8

In person, Carol Gerson proved to be less harried than she was on the phone, though she did have a frantic gleam in her eye as she marched Sabrina through the house pointing out all the necessities. "His bah-bahs are in the fridge." The toddler in her arms cooed and drooled happily.

"Bah-bahs. Fridge," Sabrina repeated. "Got it."

"And I'm so sorry there's not much food for you and your friend to snack on."

Sabrina waggled her fingers. "I'm sure I'll be able to whip something up."

"Honey, let's go," Mr. Gerson called impatiently. He wore a topcoat over his suit and held a dark cashmere coat out for his wife.

Still clutching the baby, Mrs. Gerson stuck one arm into a coat sleeve. "Now, if he gets fussy, try reading *Good Night, Moon.* He also loves to be bounced on your knee."

"Bouncie, bouncie!" Rudy squealed.

"And you'll always get a big smile when you call him Rudy Kazootie or, more formally, Mr. Kazootie." She plunged her other arm into the remaining sleeve and tapped Rudy on the nose when her hand reappeared. She was rewarded with a wet giggle.

Her husband opened the door and gestured at his wife to hurry up. But there seemed to be no end to the instructions she had to leave Sabrina. "There's his baby monitor," she said, pointing to a colorful walkie-talkie device. She held up a reclosable plastic sandwich bag. "Here are his tookies—"

"See why we need to get out?" her husband interrupted.

"We won't be home late. Call if you need anything." She flew out the door past her stunned husband. A moment later she came rushing back and placed Rudy in Sabrina's arms. "I guess you'll need this," she said. Then she was out the door again, leaving her husband holding her purse. He sighed and followed her out.

Sabrina closed the door. "So, Mr. Kazootie, what do you want to play?"

"Nose," burbled the toddler, reaching for Sabrina's face.

"Oh, that's so cute."

With the absolute single-mindedness of a baby, Rudy grabbed her nose and tugged. Hard.

An hour later there was a knock on the door. Sabrina ran toward it, then made herself slow down and open it casually. "Hi," she greeted Harvey. "You found it."

He strolled in, moving extra-casually. "Yeah. You should have just said it was the house with the flying duck on the mailbox."

"You really notice mailboxes, don't you?" said Sabrina, shaking her head.

"Yeah," Harvey said with pride. He looked at Sabrina, then at the interior of the house. "So is the baby-sitting going okay? Your nose is kind of red."

Sabrina touched it gingerly. "It's fine. The baby's asleep now. It's just the two of us." She backtracked quickly, afraid she'd said too much with that choice of words. "Not that I'd planned it that way. It's just that the baby was really tired." She was digging the hole deeper, so she abruptly changed the topic. "Look at that big TV!"

Harvey took in the huge 50-inch screen. "Wow! I'll bet the World Series game would look really great on that." With an effort, he turned back to Sabrina. "But . . . I came here to study."

"Right! So, uh, let's study." Neither Sabrina nor Harvey moved for a moment. Then they both realized they weren't moving, so they sat down at opposite ends of the couch. Harvey grinned in embarrassment. "My notes aren't very good. All I've got is 'Mitosis is . . .'"

"We can work off my notes," Sabrina said, opening her loose-leaf and scooting to the center of the couch.

Harvey eyed the diminished distance between them for a second. Then he slid over to Sabrina's side. "Okay, mitosis is . . ." The warmth from Sabrina's body tingled across his skin. He pulled back and fidgeted. "You know, studying makes me hungry."

Somewhat unnerved by the spicy tang of Harvey's aftershave, Sabrina jumped up from the couch. "Me, too. I'll see what I can dig up." She bolted for the kitchen.

A few minutes later Sabrina came back with an armload of goodies. "I found all kinds of great stuff. It's not brand name, but I'm sure it tastes fine."

Harvey sorted through the candy bars, his brow furrowed in confusion. "Shmickers? N&N's? Butterthumbs? Where do these people shop?"

Sabrina shrugged. "I don't know, but if you're thirsty they have Popsi!" She held up a blue-and-white can.

"Do they have Yoo-Hoo?"

Sabrina shuffled drinks and held up a bottle of murky brown liquid. "No, but they have Hey, Over Here."

"I think I'll just have a Diet Popsi," said Harvey, playing it safe.

"Well, we should get back to studying." Sabrina flipped open her notebook again.

Harvey moved close again, reading over her shoulder. "Okay. Mitosis is . . ."

The baby monitor slung from Sabrina's belt suddenly transmitted Rudy's cranky whimpering from upstairs. Sabrina pulled away from Harvey again. "Baby needs me. I'll be right back."

Sabrina rushed up to the baby's room. Rudy was standing in the middle of his crib, crying and pulling at his blue jumper. His eyes lit up as she approached. "It's okay, Rudy. It's okay," Sabrina soothed. She fished his book out from under a blanket. "Look, your favorite book, *Good Night, Moon.*" She riffled through the pages rapidly. "'Hello, moon, Good night moon.' That was a good book. Come on, Rudy, be a pal. Harvey and I have a study date. And don't you start 'oohing.' Although I do sorta think he's cute and . . . I don't know why I'm telling *you* this."

But Rudy had settled down with *Good Night, Moon* and was happily chewing away at the cover. "Enjoy your book," Sabrina said, closing the door gently and racing back downstairs.

The sound of the TV floated up the stairwell as Sabrina headed down. Harvey had turned it on and was watching the game. The announcer was droning, "And another quiet inning comes to an end."

"Baby's fine."

Harvey clicked off the remote and gave Sabrina a guilty look. "I was just checking the score."

Sabrina sat down on the couch next to him again. "You really like baseball, huh?"

"Yeah, but sports aren't my only interest. I don't tell a lot of people this, but someday I wanna be a dentist." Harvey was embarrassed and looked at Sabrina for approval.

She was quick to deliver. "A dentist. That's great. Who doesn't love the dentist?" she laughed. *Just when you think you know Harvey,* she thought, *he goes and drops a bomb on you.*

Harvey leaned closer. "And I've noticed you have really good teeth."

"I do?" This had nothing to do with studying, but Sabrina was thrilled—Harvey was noticing her.

"Yeah, but that's not a professional opinion. That's just me."

Rudy's cries blared from the baby monitor again. Sabrina jumped up. "Excuse me, I've gotta go to work." The TV was back on before Sabrina hit the first step.

When she entered the nursery, Rudy was wailing piteously and reaching up for someone to comfort him. Sabrina picked him up out of his crib and cuddled him, stroking his back. "Come on, Mr. Kazootie, don't be sad. Big boys don't cry. Be a big boy, be a big boy, be a big boy. . . ." The effect of her chanting was . . . well, magical. Rudy quieted down immediately and stayed quiet when Sabrina placed him gently back in the crib. He took his bottle and began sucking. "That's better. Good night, big boy."

She turned and left the room, unaware that sorcerous sparkles were snaking over the baby's body.

As she had expected, Harvey had the game back on the TV. "We go to the bottom of the ninth. What a yawner," the announcer complained. "Somebody *do* something!"

Harvey clicked the game off as Sabrina came back down the stairs. "Well, baby's got his bottle now," Sabrina said. "Shall we go back to 'mitosis is . . .'?"

"Yeah, right," said Harvey, shaking his head as if to clear it. "The test is tomorrow, so I've really gotta focus. Okay, mitosis is—"

A loud thump from the ceiling echoed through the living room.

"What was that?" yelped Sabrina.

Harvey picked up the remote again. "Better go check the baby."

Sabrina ran back upstairs and into the nursery. She took one look at Rudy and stopped dead in her tracks. "Omigod," she gasped. "Rudy, is that you?"

That was a very good question. The bottom had fallen out of Rudy's crib and hit the floor. That was what had made the thump. But the bottom had fallen out because Rudy the baby had somehow become Rudy the grown man. He sat in the wrecked crib, wearing only a blanket, reaching helplessly for his bottle, which had rolled out of his reach beyond the crib. "Bah-bah!" he demanded.

# Chapter 9

☆

Sabrina was horrified. She buried her face in her hands. "What have I done? I am in *so* much trouble. I broke the baby!"

She opened her hands and looked back at the crib. The baby in a man's body was still there. "Bah-bah," Rudy demanded.

"We have to undo this," Sabrina said in a panic. She waved her arms like a pitcher winding up and threw a point at Rudy. "Okay. Presto chango, go back to normal."

"Bah-bah."

She pointed again. "Go back to normal!"

*"Bah*-bah!"

"Oohhgh!" Sabrina battered her fists against the air. "That's not even close!"

Rudy's face scrunched up and grew very red. His mouth opened as he warmed up for a full-throated bawl. Sabrina grabbed up his bottle and thrust it into his mouth. "Okay, here's your bah-bah!"

The tension vanished out of Rudy's body. He began drinking from the bottle and smiling happily again. Sabrina was filled with despair. "This is so creepy," she moaned. "We've got to get help."

"Bankie?" offered Rudy, pulling up the corner of his coverlet.

Sabrina blanched and quickly snugged the blanket back around the child-man. "You'd better keep your bankie until we get you dressed. And I don't think anything with ducks or balloons is going to work."

Heavy footsteps on the stairs warned Sabrina of Harvey's approach. "Hey, Sabrina, you need some help?" he hollered.

Sabrina almost collided with him in her haste to keep him from coming all the way upstairs. "Nope, everything's fine. Why don't you go watch the game?"

Harvey leaned on the banister rail and jerked a lazy thumb at the TV. "It's one strike from the end. Unless this guy knocks one out, it's over."

"It can't be over!" exclaimed Sabrina. She pointed at the TV, making Harvey turn. "Hey, look—"

As soon as Harvey's eyes had left her, Sabrina pumped her fist in the air twice and pointed a spell at the players on the TV. Harvey's eyes widened at the crack of a bat. The announcer went wild. "It's a home run!" he shouted. "Out of the park! The first of his career! Folks, we're going into extra innings!"

"Unbelievable!" Harvey muttered, stumbling downstairs to take up his seat on the couch again.

Sabrina raced back upstairs to the Gersons' bedroom to look in Jerry Gerson's closet for some suitable clothes. Trailing a loaded hanger, she ran into the nursery.

In not-so-short order, she had Rudy dressed in a shirt, pants, and a jacket. "You could help a little," she complained as she struggled to get his arm through the jacket sleeve.

When his hand appeared at the end of the sleeve, Rudy kept it going to grab for Sabrina's face. "Nose," he cackled.

"Oww!" she yowled, pulling quickly away. "That's not helping. Stay still. There. Hey, you look pretty cute. Just don't spit up on your dad's suit, okay?" Sabrina stood up and stretched, trying to relax and maintain control of the situation.

Rudy sat on the floor, his hands raised toward Sabrina. "Up?"

"You've gotta be kidding me," she said.

Just then the phone rang. Sabrina patted Rudy on the head, hoping he would stay, like a dog. "Gotta go answer the phone."

Jerry Gerson's dream of a quiet evening out was in danger of becoming a nightmare. His wife couldn't seem to relax and enjoy dinner. She kept fretting and worrying about how their son was doing at home. Never mind that this was practically the first time he and Carol had been alone together since Rudy was born. So now he was here on the pay phone, calling his own home, with his wife hanging on to his arm.

"Did she answer yet?" Carol Gerson asked anxiously.

"Am I talking?" he snapped back.

The phone at the house was picked up. "Hi, Sabrina? It's Jerry, Rudy's dad."

"Is he okay?" Carol nagged. "Ask her if he's okay."

Jerry shot his wife a dirty look. "I know what to ask," he growled under his breath. Then, in a normal voice, he asked Sabrina, "Is he okay?"

"Yeah!" Sabrina returned cheerfully. "Rudy's having a real good time! He's riding his banana right now. How's your dinner?"

"They were a little late in seating us," Jerry began.

"Really!" exclaimed Sabrina.

"But since we got a table they've been rushing the heck out of us."

Sabrina sounded upset to hear this. "Oh, don't let them," she told him. "You're there to relax. Take all the time you want."

Jerry was surprised and pleased. "Why, that's very sweet of you, Sabrina." He shot a glance at his wife. "Well, we were just checking in. See you soon." He almost missed the baby-sitter's answer. "Okay, not *too* soon. Right. Bye."

Jerry hung up the phone and turned to his wife. "See?" he said. "Everything's fine."

Carol unbent slowly and leaned into his chest. "I'm sorry. It's just been such a weird day. I mean, you almost went off the road in that freak snowstorm—and now I have just the funniest feeling."

Jerry took her by the shoulders and steered her back to their table. "Stop with the feelings," he muttered, but not loud enough for his wife to hear.

Sabrina poked her head around the corner of the stairwell to make sure that Harvey was locked into the game. Sure enough, he was sitting on the edge of the couch, his eyes glued to the screen. "Harvey, I'm going to walk the baby. You stay here and watch the game, okay?"

" 'Kay," Harvey tried to say around a mouthful of Butterthumbs. "But it's almost over. Only a grand slam would tie this game."

Sabrina pumped her fist twice in the air and pointed at the TV. Harvey leaned forward in open-mouthed wonder as the announcer called out the sudden change in play: "The bases are loaded as Patton hikes the lumber. Here's the pitch. And it's up . . . it's hanging there . . . it's hanging there . . . it could be . . . it might be . . . it's a *grand slam!*"

"All right!" Harvey crowed.

With her study date occupied, Sabrina ran down the stairs, dragging Rudy along by one arm. She opened the front door and pulled Rudy outside. As she left, she heard the TV announcer proclaim, "There's magic in the air!"

"Welcome, parents. I'm Mr. Pool and this is biology." The lanky teacher underscored his name on the chalkboard. He turned and smiled broadly at his audience. With his beaky face and prominent Adam's apple, he reminded many of his listeners of Ichabod Crane. "Tonight we're here to talk about your kids. Now, I know you look in their faces and see the hopes and dreams of the future. But I see only blank, insipid stares, taunting me. So why am I, a man in my prime, teaching high school biology? Well, I believe that science is the foundation upon which we build our future. That, and I tanked my MCATs."

Zelda leaned over to whisper in Hilda's ear, "Mr. Pool is cute."

Hilda stared at her sister in disbelief. "You have *got* to get out more."

Zelda's eyes misted over. "I wonder if he's single."

"Excuse me," Mr. Pool interrupted, staring right at them. "Is there something you'd like to share with the rest of the class?"

"I need to go to the nurse," Hilda piped up.

Mr. Pool stalked closer. "Is there a problem"— he bent forward to read Hilda's press-on name tag—"Mrs. Spellman?"

Hilda started to answer, "Yes, my tummy—"

Zelda silenced her with a sharp squeeze on the

wrist. "She's fine," Zelda insisted, "and it's *Miss* Spellman." She favored him with a dazzling smile.

"Who are you?" asked Pool, puzzled, but already trapped by that smile.

"I'm also Miss Spellman. We're Sabrina's aunts." Then Zelda rushed to add, "We're sisters, not an alternative couple."

Pool straightened up and waggled his eyebrows slightly. "So you're single?"

"Yes," breathed Zelda. "And you?"

"Extremely!"

Hilda turned away, looking ill. "Now I really *am* gonna throw up," she muttered.

Sabrina led Rudy into the Spellman kitchen. She had his diaper bag slung over one shoulder. "In here, Rudy. And please get your finger out of your nose."

Rudy pulled his finger out and reached for Sabrina's nose. "Nose," he demanded.

Sabrina ducked out of his reach. "Gross. Leave mine alone. Just sit down and don't get into any trouble." She pushed him into a chair and stuffed *Good Night, Moon* into his hands. "Here, you can read your book."

Rudy promptly stuck the book in his mouth and started chewing on it.

"Or just chew on it." Sabrina left him and went into the dining room, looking for the cat.

She found Salem on the dining room table, a place he knew he wasn't supposed to go, attacking a ball of pink yarn. With each pounce he yelled, "Yes! Yes! Yes!"

"Salem, what are you doing?"

The cat froze, a pink thread looped around one fang. "Nothing."

Sabrina moved forward and loomed over the cat. "It looks like you're playing with a ball of yarn."

"I have urges, Sabrina. I'm a man, but I'm also a cat!"

This was almost as unappealing as Rudy and his finger. Sabrina scooped the cat up from the table. "Salem, can we deal with your issues later? I've got bigger problems. Come."

"My yarn," whined Salem as they left the room and returned to the kitchen.

Rudy was flapping the covers of his book like a bird when Sabrina carried Salem past and set him on the island. "Oh, dear Lord, you picked up a guy at the bus station," said the cat.

"No, he's the baby I'm baby-sitting. He's four-teen months old. Something happened to him."

"Do I smell teen witchery?" Salem sneered.

"Maybe. Yes." Sabrina felt overwhelmed. She threw herself on the mercy of the cat. "Help me, Salem. We've got to change him back before his parents get home and prosecute."

"What do you want from me? I'm only a cat. Go talk to your aunts."

Sabrina was at her wits' end. "But they're at my school," she wailed in frustration. "I can't take him there. Can you watch him?"

"I suppose," Salem said grudgingly.

Sabrina picked the cat up and carried him over to the table. "Thanks, I owe you one."

A soon as Rudy laid eyes on the cat, however, he reached out for the feline, squealing happily, "Horsey! Ride horsey!"

He got his stubby fingers around Salem's middle and made as if to climb astride the cat. Salem bolted at the first opportunity, scrabbling across the tile floor and yelling, "Get him out of here! Get him out of here!"

Sabrina watched the cat disappear. She suddenly had a sinking feeling in her stomach. She'd have to take Rudy to school after all.

☆

# Chapter 10

☆

Zelda leaned over the Formica top of the lab table, her eyes locked with Mr. Pool's. She laughed throatily. "What an amusing Erlenmeyer flask story, Mr. Pool."

"Really?" He blushed at her praise. "I've told it a thousand times and no one's ever gotten it."

Zelda shook her head sadly. "Fools!"

Mr. Pool nearly bloomed under such intense attention. "Thanks. I just can't get over how much you know about science," he marveled.

"Well, I am a theoretical chemical physicist with degrees from M.I.T. and CalTech," Zelda murmured modestly.

"Really?"

"I was even on the short list for the Nobel last year." Zelda noticed he was wilting, a clear sign that he was feeling overmatched. She switched topics and bubbled, "You know, we should exchange E-mail. What's your address?"

The question took Pool by surprise. "Me? I, uh . . . I'm on QuikNet." He swaggered a little. "My screen name is BioStud."

"*You're* BioStud?" Zelda squealed, clapping her hands together. "I'm ChemKitten!"

"Didn't we meet in a chat room discussion of polyvinylchlorides?"

"Yes. And you are *very* naughty!"

Hilda was ready to toss her cookies by now. All the other adults had moved on to other classrooms and other teachers, but because Zelda was flirting with this nerd, Hilda was bored and losing all patience. She levitated a piece of chalk and wrote "Loser" on the blackboard behind Pool, drawing out the tail of the *r* so that it became an arrow pointing at the science teacher. She made the chalk underscore "Loser" heavily, and the screeching sound it made on the blackboard caused both Zelda and Pool to jump suddenly.

Mr. Pool had turned around and was staring in befuddlement at the writing on the board when Sabrina poked her head into the classroom and tried quietly to get her aunts' attention.

"Hey, Sabrina!" Hilda greeted her niece.

"Sabrina? What are you doing at Parents' Night?" Mr. Pool tore his eyes from the board and stared at his student. One mystery at a time was all he could handle.

"Nothing," she said. "I just—"

Mr. Pool caught sight of Rudy outside the door. "Ah, you brought your father." He opened the door full width. Rudy toddled in and was immediately drawn to a mobile of the solar system.

"Moon," he said, reaching up to touch Jupiter.

Sabrina grabbed his sleeve and pulled the pudgy hand back. "Ah! Don't play with that . . . Dad."

"Nice to meet you, Mr. Spellman." Mr. Pool tried to shake Rudy's hand, but the baby-man ignored him and went back to reaching for the moon. "Mr. Spellman?"

Sabrina took Mr. Pool by the arm and whispered confidentially, "Actually, he likes to be called Mr. Kazootie."

"Mr. Kazootie?"

"Yeah, that's our real name. It's, uh . . . Scottish." Sabrina smiled weakly at her teacher. "You can see why we changed it."

Mr. Pool straightened up and affected an atrocious imitation of a Scottish burr. "I'm Scottish, too, but I know naught of the Clan Kazootie. Be ye a Highlander?"

"Plbblt!" Rudy blew a raspberry at him.

Sabrina tugged Mr. Pool by the arm again, pulling him away from Rudy. "We're Lowlanders," she assured him.

Pool wasn't quite convinced. "Is your dad okay, Sabrina?" he asked. Before she could answer, the teacher's digital watch emitted a shrill beep. Pool looked down and saw the time. "Oh, darn! I've got to work the bake sale." His eye caught Zelda's and he puffed out his chest. "It's a prestige thing," he told her.

Zelda came up and stood close to him. Very close. "You do it all, don't you?" she breathed.

Mr. Pool leaned stiffly forward to whisper a secret to her. "I've got to hop, but come by and I'll slip you a Rice Krispie treat."

"Snap, crackle, and pop," said Zelda coquettishly. Pool floated out of the room, his feet not even near the floor. This wasn't sorcery; this was magic of an earthier sort.

Hilda took Pool's departure as permission to breathe normally again. "Aren't you supposed to be baby-sitting?" she asked Sabrina.

"I am. That's him." Sabrina pointed at Rudy.

*"That's* the little baby?" exclaimed Hilda with a short laugh. "No wonder they have trouble finding sitters."

Rudy smiled at Hilda. "Funny clown."

"Watch it," she growled.

Sabrina shouted to regain her aunts' attention. "Look, I'm desperate! You guys have to help me! His parents will be back really soon, and I think they might notice that they missed a big moment in their son's life!" She was pacing back and forth.

Zelda tried logic first. "Well, obviously you cast some kind of spell. All you have to do is reverse it."

Sabrina felt her mind spin with confusion and frustration. "What spell? I didn't cast a spell. Or at least I didn't mean to. This magic ruins everything! He's supposed to be in his crib, sucking his thumb, and I'm supposed to be studying with Harvey right now!"

"Ohhh . . ." said Zelda.

"Uh-huh . . ." Hilda winked.

Sabrina blew her top. *"Stop that!"* she shouted. "This is *serious!*"

Logic hadn't helped much, so Zelda tried reason. "Calm down, Sabrina. Now, you must have said *something."*

Sabrina took a deep breath, trying to calm herself and clear her memory. "I don't know! I don't remember! Rudy was crying, so I picked him up. I said, 'Big boys don't cry'—I know it's not P.C.—and then I rubbed his back."

"Did you say anything else?"

"I don't remember," Sabrina repeated.

"Be a big boy," offered Rudy from the corner, where he was prying apart a plastic brain.

Sabrina whirled and pointed at Rudy. "That's it!"

Zelda's face lit up with understanding. "And I'll bet you said it three times?" she asked, but it was clear she already knew the answer.

Hilda caught the ball and drove it home. "Ah! Mystery solved. You cast a passion spell."

"What's a passion spell?" demanded Sabrina.

Zelda tried to explain the workings of emotional magic. "If you want something bad enough and say it three times, it can happen."

Hilda smiled fondly. "We like to call it a Travis."

"A Travis?" asked Sabrina. "Why?"

By way of answer, Zelda closed her eyes and chanted slowly, "Randy Travis. Randy Travis. Randy Travis."

She waved her hand at the blackboard and there, suddenly standing in front of it, was Randy Travis, the country-western singer.

"I love this spell." Hilda sighed, gazing at him.

Travis blinked at his unexpected surroundings. "What am I doing here?"

Zelda shone her brightest smile at him. "Oh, we were just illustrating a point for our niece. I hope we haven't caught you at a bad time."

"No, it's fine," Travis replied. "My wife does wonder where I keep poppin' off to, though. Will there be anything else?"

"Maybe later." Hilda smirked mischievously.

Travis shrugged his shoulders and headed for the door. "If you need me, you'll know where to find me. You always do."

Hilda bit her knuckle. "Grrrr! Now *he* is cute!"

"And I just love his latest album," Zelda sighed.

"Can we get back to me?" Sabrina interrupted petulantly. "What do I do to fix *this?*" She waved at Rudy, who was now trying to eat the plastic brain.

Zelda took her niece by the shoulders and turned her to face Rudy. "Exactly what you did before, three times, but in reverse."

"This is really weird," Sabrina said. She rubbed Rudy's back and chanted, "Boy big a be, boy big a be, boy big a be."

Rudy laughed uproariously. "Tickle!" he squealed.

Sabrina stepped back to look at him. "Nothing happened! It didn't work."

"Don't worry," said Zelda. "It takes some time."

"It's always harder to take off weight than it is to put it on," Hilda observed.

Sabrina slid back into despair. "But his parents are going to be home soon!"

"You'd better hope they have a sense of humor," cracked Hilda.

"Maybe I can blame it on a radioactive spider?" Sabrina wondered aloud as she slumped in hopeless despair against the table.

Zelda leaned over to whisper loudly into Sabrina's ear. "So . . . does Mr. Pool have a girlfriend?"

The very idea made Sabrina shudder uneasily. "I seriously doubt it. Why?"

"She," said Hilda, nodding her head in her sister's direction, "was flirting with him." She pointed out the door. "Big time."

"Please," Zelda objected. "We were just exchanging scientific ideas."

Hilda straightened up in order to contradict Zelda better. "You were batting your eyelashes enough to spell 'take me' in Morse code."

"I did no such—"

"Oh, you did too."

"I was merely enjoying his company."

"You were discussing sex genes!"

Once again it took Sabrina yelling at the top of her lungs to stop the bickering. "Guys, could you argue about this later? It's really embarrassing."

"Hey, look!" said Hilda, pointing to the spot where Rudy had been. And wasn't any longer.

"Rudy! Rudy!" called Sabrina. The three Spellman witches went running after the enchanted child with Sabrina in the lead, yelling, "Where's the baby?"

Down the hall in the cafeteria, Mr. Pool, impressed to the soles of his feet by the honor of serving Randy Travis, was holding out a brownie in a trembling hand. "It's on the house, Mr. Travis."

Travis took the brownie and examined it suspiciously. "Does it have nuts?"

"Yes . . . but you can pick them out," Mr. Pool said helpfully.

Rudy chose that moment to toddle into the room. He took one look at the baked goods spread out on the table in front of Mr. Pool and gleefully shouted, "Tookies!"

Rudy threw himself at the table, grabbing as many cupcakes, cookies, and brownies as he could, stuffing them all in his mouth, his eyes wide with delight.

Mr. Pool was outraged. "Hey, you can't—" he shouted to the man-baby.

"Mine!" pouted Rudy, his face a smear of chocolate and icing.

Mr. Pool pointed an accusing finger at Rudy and thundered in his best Tough Teacher voice, *"Mister Kazootie!"*

Sabrina and her aunts made it to the cafeteria just in time to see Rudy turn red and burst into tears.

☆

# Chapter 11

☆

Sabrina sneaked Rudy back into the Gerson house as the TV announcer declared, "It's the bottom of the fifteenth. Put on a pot of java. We could be here all night!"

She slunk up the stairs, hoping Harvey would be too absorbed in the game to notice her. She came close to getting caught. Harvey didn't turn his head away from the screen, but he did call out, "Sabrina, is that you?"

"Yeah," she answered, pushing a very tired Rudy as fast as she could up the steps. *If only I can get him back before his parents arrive,* she thought. That was the only thing in her mind at this point.

"You're missing a freaky game," Harvey said.

Sabrina winced. *That's what you think!*

Sabrina found a pair of Jerry Gerson's pajamas in the linen closet. After a lot of tugging on her part and nose-pulling on Rudy's part, she managed to get the baby-man into them. Then she coaxed him back into his broken crib and he snuggled down with his bankie. "You've had a big night," she told him softly. "Now it's time to go over what I taught you. Rudy, how did you get this way?"

Rudy lifted his hands, palms up, as if to say, Who knows?

"Good. Now it's sleepy time."

Rudy held up *Good Night, Moon.* "Wead me. Moon."

Sabrina sagged. "I'm too tired. Play with your toes." She clipped the baby monitor back on her belt and trudged downstairs.

She staggered over to the couch, collapsing on it when she got there. She reached for the blue can on the coffee table. "I could sure use a Popsi. Is the game still on?"

"Yeah," said Harvey in rapt fascination, eyes glued to the TV screen. "And it could go on forever."

It was time to end the magic-play for the night. Sabrina pumped her fist twice and pointed at the TV. The announcer screamed, "It's an unassisted triple play! It's over!"

"Wow," breathed Harvey. "That's what's so great about baseball. Anything can happen."

"Yeah, yeah," said Sabrina flatly. "You never know."

Harvey took Sabrina's terseness as a veiled jab at the supposed point of their evening together. He snatched up the loose-leaf and said quickly, "We really should study now. Mitosis is . . ."

"You know, could we take a break? This baby-sitting is a lot harder than I thought." *And I don't want to think anymore tonight,* her brain whined.

"Sure," said Harvey, putting down the notebook. "I mean, we could just sit here and talk."

Sabrina smiled at him. "I'd like that." She scootched a little closer to him.

"This is kind of nice," Harvey said, moving a little closer to her.

"Yeah."

"So . . ."

"So . . ." The tension between them grew. The air seemed to become thicker, magnifying their faces.

The front door swung open. "We're home!" sang the Gersons.

Harvey leaped a yard backward from Sabrina. "Mitosis is!" he shouted in panic.

Sabrina popped up to greet her employers. "I didn't expect you so soon."

"We skipped dessert," Carol explained. "I missed my baby so much."

"I hope he wasn't any trouble," said Jerry.

"Not at all," Sabrina quickly assured them, trying to gather up all her stuff at once.

Jerry fished his wallet out of his pocket. "So how much do we owe you? Four dollars an hour?"

Sabrina had finally found her coat and gotten Harvey to move toward the door. "Actually, it'.

five." She watched nervously as Carol started up the stairs. It was time to split—pronto! "But four would be fine," she said, grabbing the money out of Jerry's hand and pulling Harvey out the door. "Thanks. Gotta go."

Jerry Gerson was puzzled by Sabrina's haste, but didn't dwell on it. One thought—*Kids!*—seemed to cover all bases. His wife called to him from the nursery. "Jerry, you've got to come see this!"

He joined his wife at the door to the nursery. Through the darkness they could barely make out the shape of their son, snuggled into his blankets.

"Look at our sweet little angel," Carol murmured.

Jerry gazed at the little bundle in the crib. "They grow so quickly, don't they?"

Carol looked up at him with wide, dreaming eyes. "Did you ever think about, you know, having another?"

The thought of ten years or more before having another night alone with his wife made Jerry Gerson yelp "No!" before he could stop himself. He patted Carol on the shoulder. "We should go now."

As Sabrina tiptoed into her home, she saw that the kitchen light was on. Slipping up to the doorway, she saw Randy Travis working on a jigsaw puzzle with her aunts. Randy said, "I'm lookin' for a slanty green piece with a funny little wattle."

"Here you go," offered Hilda.

"Thank you."

Zelda leaned forward and flashed a hundred-watt smile. "You know, you really have a flair for jigsaw puzzles, Randy."

"I spend a lotta time on the bus."

Hilda crinkled her eyes at him. "This is kind of nice, though. Popcorn. Puzzle. Lightly falling snow."

"It's real nice," agreed Travis. "Can I go now?"

"No!" both women said in unison.

Travis sighed, accepting his temporary fate. "Okay. Lookin' for a sky-blue rhombus with a little puff of clouds. Oh, here it is."

Sabrina chuckled to herself and quietly went upstairs.

Salem was grooming himself on the bed when Sabrina came in and set her notebook down on the desk. He ignored her entrance in favor of nipping at a particularly itchy spot at the base of his tail.

Sabrina tried to work up enough concentration to study, getting as far as "Mitosis is . . ." before being distracted by memories of the evening's troubles. But more importantly, she remembered her closeness to Harvey. Why did boys have to cloud her mind so?

Thinking of boys and remembering Randy Travis downstairs brought another thought to the forefront of her mind. *I just* have *to try that trick,* Sabrina thought. But first she had to get rid of gossipy witnesses.

"Salem! I think I hear the can opener!"

That got a rise out of the cat. "Really?" He jumped off the bed and raced out the door, crying, "Please be tuna! Please be tuna!"

Sabrina rushed to the mirror and smoothed her outfit down. Then she concentrated and chanted, "Eddie Cibrian. Eddie Cibrian. Eddie Cibrian."

An instant later the darkly handsome *Baywatch Nights* star stood in front of Sabrina. She gawked at him. Oh, this was too cool!

But he just looked confused. "Uh, what am I doing here? I was just about to pull Hasselhoff out of a burning Corvette."

Sabrina practiced her own luminous smile. She made it to about fifty watts. "Oh, well, you can do that later. I was just wondering if you could turn around for me."

Cibrian raised his eyebrows but said, "Sure."

"Thanks." Sabrina nearly hopped up and down for joy as the T-shirt and jeans–clad hunk spun slowly in front of her.

"Is that it?"

"Yeah," Sabrina said almost apologetically. "Unless you're into jigsaw puzzles. My aunts are downstairs right now working on one with Randy Travis."

Cibrian pursed his lips in thought. "Sounds like fun," he decided. "Guess Hasselhoff will have to wait." He walked on down the stairs.

Sabrina found herself shivering from the thrill.

She congratulated herself on her sorcerous success. "Guess this magic thing isn't bad."

*Why not go for broke, then?* she thought. She closed her eyes and chanted, "Brad Pitt. Brad Pitt. Brad Pitt."

Alas, as Sabrina had already found out, there were some things magic *couldn't* do.

☆

# Chapter 12

☆

The next day, Sabrina sat in biology class watching Mr. Pool pass out the test papers. He handed the last one out and then announced, "You have the test. You may commence failing."

Across the room, she could hear Harvey muttering to himself, "Mitosis is . . . mitosis is . . ."

Mr. Pool apparently heard it too. He strolled over to Harvey and said cheerfully, "Great game last night, eh, Harvey?"

Harvey's head popped up and he grinned. "Oh, yeah!" Then he realized that Mr. Pool had made him admit that he'd watched the ball game instead of studying. He buried his head in the test again, muttering, "Mitosis is . . ."

Sabrina looked around the classroom, at the teacher, at the students. It was sinking into her brain that this was her life for the next four years.

These people and her family were nearly everyone she had to deal with.

Her social life revolved around Jenny and Harvey and the crowd who hung out at the Slicery, the local pizza joint. For some reason, though, Sabrina's name was at the top of Libby's spite list, and the cheerleader and her loyal troop of fashion slaves took every opportunity to make sure that Sabrina knew she was still an outsider.

It was more fun to think about Jenny and Harvey. Especially Harvey.

For all his good looks and amiable personality, Sabrina couldn't understand why Harvey didn't take charge of his life in a more active way. He seemed to cheerfully go along with whatever other people expected of him. At home, this meant that he kept trying to live up to his sports-mad father's dream of Harvey-the-champion-athlete. At school, he waited until someone else made a decision and then hopped on board for the ride.

This wasn't good enough for Sabrina. She wanted Harvey to notice her, but there was no way on earth that she could simply *tell* him to do that. So every day was a trial of patience, waiting for him to wake up and notice how she felt about him. Last night they had come so close to exposing their feelings. . . .

Sabrina was not going to let this relationship slide. With the first dance of the school year, the Harvest Dance, only a week away, she felt that it was time for Harvey to make his move. But how could she possibly make *him* realize that?

At home that afternoon, Sabrina realized that she'd been spending a lot of time staring at the phone lately, willing Harvey to call her. When the phone did ring, she was always the first to snatch it up, which meant some hazardous near-misses with Salem's tail as she raced through the house.

Her aunt Zelda was making a cup of tea that afternoon. Just an ordinary, everyday thing, if your taste in tea included a brew that bubbled and smoked in the cup. The phone on the kitchen wall rang. By now Zelda had learned not even to bother getting up.

Sure enough, Sabrina yelled down the stairs, "It's for me!" and came galloping into the kitchen to grab the handset off the hook. "Hello?" Her look of desperation melted into a silly smile. "Hi, Harvey. Sure, ask away."

Then she noticed her aunt sitting at the island, beaming fondly at her. "Just a sec," Sabrina said into the phone. She put her hand over the mouthpiece and glared at her aunt. "Aunt Zelda, do you mind?"

Zelda sipped at her tea. "Oh, no, go right ahead," she said.

Sometimes adults could be so clueless! "I mean, would you leave me alone?" Sabrina asked pointedly.

"Oh, I get it," said Zelda, obviously not really

getting it. "Sorry." She sailed gracefully out of the kitchen, her tea trailing vapor as she left.

Sabrina removed her hand from the phone's mouthpiece. "You were saying . . .?" she prompted, hoping this would be the big moment.

Just then a very grumpy Hilda came stomping into the kitchen. "Out of my way," she grumbled. "I'm hungry."

"Hold on, Harvey." Sabrina jabbed a finger at the table, and a sandwich appeared on a plate. "That's to go," Sabrina told her aunt, motioning her to pick up the sandwich and leave. "I'm talking to Harvey."

Hilda picked up the sandwich but didn't leave. "About what?" she asked.

Sabrina sighed in exasperation. "I won't know until I get some privacy!"

"I'm going, I'm going." Hilda peeled back the bread on the sandwich. "Is this pressed turkey?" Sabrina glared, and thunder rattled the sky outside the house. "I'm going!" Hilda yelped and vanished with her sandwich into the dining room.

Sabrina composed herself and turned back to the phone. "You had a question?"

"Hee-hee-hee!" came a high-pitched cackle from the picnic basket on the island.

"One more sec," Sabrina told Harvey. She glared at the basket. "Salem! Are you spying on me?"

Salem poked his head out of the basket. "I'm a cat," he drawled. "I'm curious. So kill me."

106

*"Out!"*

"Fine. I understand the delicacy of the moment." Salem leaped out of the basket and trotted away, chanting, "Harvey and Sabrina, Harvey and Sabrina!"

Sabrina took a deep breath to calm herself and then returned to the phone. *Oh, Harvey, please, please, please ask me to the dance!* "You were saying . . .?" Her face fell as she listened. "No, Mr. Pool said photosynthesis would *not* be on the test. Is that it?" Apparently it was. "Okay, Harvey, see you tomorrow."

Sabrina hung up the phone and leaned into the corner, her head resting on the frame of the portrait of a woman in mid-nineteenth-century dress.

The painting's lips moved. "There, there. I'm sure Harvey will ask you out on a date someday."

"Thanks, Louisa," Sabrina automatically answered. Then her eyes widened in shock and outrage. "You were listening? I have no privacy in this house!"

Sabrina ran to her room, Louisa's high-pitched chant of "Harvey and Sabrina, Harvey and Sabrina!" following her up the stairs. Magical creatures were weird enough to begin with, but why did they all seem to be so *juvenile?*

At lunch the next day in the cafeteria, Sabrina stared glumly at Libby and one of the lesser fashion zombies, Sasha, as they hung bunting over a large banner announcing the Harvest Dance. She overheard Sasha say to Libby, "I just don't get how people can dance with all these tables here."

For a brief moment Sabrina actually sympathized with Libby as the cheerleader stared with disbelief at her bubble-headed helper. "Sasha," Libby said slowly, "we'll *move* the tables."

"We can do that?" Sasha said, honestly surprised.

Libby's ego outweighed her scorn. "We're the dance committee. We can do whatever we want."

Sabrina was marveling at the almost universal shortage of common sense in the world when Jenny dropped into the seat next to her. Jenny was bubbling over with excitement about something, her curly red hair dancing around her face. "It looks like I'm going to the dance," she declared.

*Wow,* Sabrina thought. As different as Sabrina felt in school, Jenny practically made a career out of being an outsider and a nonconformist. "Who with?" she asked.

"Me," Jenny announced. "I was in line waiting for my pizza when it hit me—dates are just society's way of keeping numbers even. I'm going to represent all things that are odd." She beamed at Sabrina, glowing with satisfaction at her novel conclusion.

Sabrina stifled a laugh. "And that's exactly how people will see it," she said tactfully.

"Hey, you want to come with me? We could go alone together!"

"No, thanks," Sabrina said, trying not to think her way through that pretzel logic. "Actually, I was thinking it might be fun to go with Harvey."

"Good idea. You can destroy the system from within." Sabrina cocked an eyebrow at this. Jenny babbled on without noticing. "So are you going to ask him?"

"I can't. I don't want to complicate our friendship."

"What if he asks you?"

Sabrina grinned. "Oh, I don't mind if *he* complicates our friendship."

"I see," said Jenny. The two girls laughed. Then Jenny suddenly popped up out of her chair, waving across the cafeteria and shouting, "Hey, Harvey— over here!"

Harvey sauntered over, carrying a serving of pizza on his tray. "Thanks for waving. I might not have spotted you at the same table where we always sit."

Jenny ignored his sarcasm. "So do you have plans for the dance tomorrow night? Oops, got to run!" She was out the door in a flash.

"I've never seen her move so fast," said Harvey, puzzled.

Sabrina took the opening that Jenny had set up for her. "You were saying about the dance?"

Harvey shrugged and gave Sabrina a silly smile. "I probably won't go. School dances aren't my thing. How about you?"

"I hadn't made any plans." Then, thinking she might have sent the wrong signal, she added, "You know, yet."

"Hi, Harvey. Could I borrow a finger?" Libby appeared beside Harvey, holding out the neck of an inflated balloon. Sabrina was convinced that Libby possessed not only built-in Harvey radar but also an exquisite gift for appearing when Sabrina least wanted to see her.

Harvey, of course, was blind to the feminine duel going on around him. "Sure," he said genially. He stuck out his index finger so Libby could tie a knot in the balloon.

"Excuse me. We were talking. Other people have fingers, too, you know." Sabrina's words were sharp enough to pop the balloon.

"But Harvey works out." Libby's voice purred, but her eyes shot daggers of scorn. She turned her attention back to Harvey and poured on the charm. "And by the way, Harvey, I was thinking . . . you and I could go to the dance together, okay?"

Harvey blinked in surprise. "Okay," he said automatically.

"Great. Thanks for helping." Libby beamed triumphantly at Sabrina before sauntering back to the banner on the wall.

" 'Okay'?" Sabrina almost shouted. "I thought you said that school dances weren't your thing."

Harvey looked confused and embarrassed. "They're not. I panicked." He frowned in thought. "I have a hard time saying no. I really should work on that." He raised his finger and tried to sound stern. "No. No," he rehearsed.

*He's hopeless!* thought Sabrina.

Harvey underscored her point by telling her, "If you're lucky, no one will ask you."

*Completely hopeless.*

At home that night Sabrina stood before her desk and flipped through the pages of her magic book. Zelda walked past the door, carrying an armload of towels bound for the linen closet.

"Aunt Zelda, I need help," Sabrina called out.

"Well, of course. What is it?" Zelda put the towels away and walked into Sabrina's bedroom.

"Well, it's kind of private . . ."

"Did someone say 'private'?" Hilda said cheer-ily, popping her head around the edge of the door.

"Yes," Sabrina said pointedly.

Hilda bounced in. "I'm intrigued. Continue."

"Okay. I'll tell you my problem, but I'm not using any real names." Sabrina moved to sit on her bed with one aunt on either side of her. "I wanted to go to the dance tonight with this guy—"

"Harvey," Zelda said knowingly.

Sabrina blinked. "Right," she continued slowly. "But he's going with this other girl—"

"Libby," Hilda filled in.

Sabrina jumped up. Obviously her aunts knew all about her private business. "Okay. And *then* what happens?" she snapped.

Zelda tried to calm her niece. "Oh, sweetie, if Harvey likes Libby, then that's his choice."

"But I don't think he does." How could Sabrina explain the situation? *"She* asked *him.* And because he has a problem saying no, he said yes!"

"Then why didn't *you* ask him?" Hilda said bluntly, standing to face Sabrina.

"Because then he would know that I liked him." *Duh,* Sabrina added silently.

"But you do."

Didn't her aunt get it? "Yes. But I can't tell *him* that."

Zelda, more patient than her sister, stepped between them. "Have you at least dropped a hint?"

Sabrina shrugged and looked down. "Well, I smile at him a lot . . . and sometimes when we play Foosball, I let him win."

Zelda adopted the voice of age and experience. "He'll never figure it out that way. Sixteen-year-old boys are oblivious. If you like Harvey, you have to tell him."

"You may even want to use one of these," Hilda said, conjuring a heavy object into Sabrina's hands.

"A sledgehammer?" Sabrina said, struggling to hold the massive block of iron on a stick. She failed, and the sledgehammer dropped to the floor. Silently thanking the cosmos for sparing her toes, she stepped over to her desk. "Look, I'd rather just use a love spell," she said, flipping pages in her book. "But I can't seem to find one in my magic book."

"Sabrina, I hate to disappoint you, but there *is*

no love spell," said Zelda. "Love is far too precious to tamper with."

"You mean, too weird," Hilda corrected. "That's why there's no standard formula. Although Calvin Klein came remarkably close"—she leaned close to Sabrina to whisper—"with Obsession."

This was not what Sabrina wanted to hear. She slammed the book closed and stalked over to her bed, plunking herself down on it. "So being a witch doesn't help me at all?"

"In this case, no." Zelda tried to be gentle.

As always, Hilda had a different spin on the subject. "Not necessarily. You can't *make* someone love you." She held out her right hand to flash a ring with a gaudy stone set in it. "But you *can* imprison him in a ring for *not* loving you. See?"

Deep inside the stone Sabrina could make out the minuscule figure of a man in a Elizabethan doublet, pantaloons, and hose. He felt their attention, and his tiny bearded mouth moved. "Hilda, let me out!" Sabrina heard faintly. "Thou art starting to grow on me!"

Hilda bent her hand back to admire the ring. "I just love the way he catches the light."

It was obvious to Sabrina that familial advice was not going to help. "Look," she told her aunts. "Trapping Harvey in amber is not what I had in mind. I think I need to be alone again."

Neither aunt moved. Sabrina got up from the bed and threw herself into the overstuffed chair by the window. She rested her chin on her fist.

"Oh!" Hilda sounded like a schoolchild re
minded of a lesson. "That privacy thing?"

Zelda took charge. "Hilda, let's go." She adde
as she left, "We'll be downstairs if you need us."

Hilda backed out of the room, smiling at Sa
brina. "That's right. We're here. We care. And w
have pie."

Once outside the room, Hilda closed the doo
and turned to glare at her older sister. "Tha
stinks," she declared.

Zelda agreed, if in a more formal way. "Harve
or no Harvey, Sabrina should go to the ball—
mean, the dance."

Hilda lit up with an idea. "Maybe she could g
with Raphael?"

The wee voice inside the ring cried out shrilly, "
can trip the light fantastic!"

Hilda shook her hand dismissively. The rin
hand. "No. He's too out of touch. Sabrina need
someone hip and fun who will make her forge
Harvey."

Zelda pondered. Then she looked slyly at Hilda
"I know! Do we have any Man-Doh in the house?"

Hilda grew excited. "Great idea! I'll race you t
the kitchen!"

☆

# Chapter 13

☆

The two women, soberly dressed and certainly old enough to be considered adults, jostled each other down the stairs, elbows flying and hips bumping. They reached the bottom of the stairs simultaneously, but Hilda sprinted down the hallway to enter the kitchen a step ahead of Zelda.

Hilda strutted like an Olympic winner. "Beat you!"

"Oh, you are *so* immature," Zelda said petulantly.

Salem sat like a statue in the middle of the kitchen table. He twitched his whiskers a fraction. "Do you mind? I'm busy staring into space."

Hilda scooped Salem up from the table and spun around with the cat in her arms. "You can do that later. We're making Sabrina a dream date!"

She put the cat down on the island and went back

to clear the table off as Zelda opened up a secret cabinet hidden behind Louisa's portrait. She started taking out colored bottles of magical ingredients.

Soon a large linen-covered board dusted with flour was sitting on the table. In an enormous bowl, Hilda kneaded a huge lump of dough, occasionally adding more powdered mix from a large yellow-and-white box labeled "No-bake Man-Doh." Zelda had set the oddly shaped colored glass bottles along the island and was rolling out a batch of dough with a rolling pin. Both women had donned crisp Donna Reed aprons.

When the dough was rolled thin enough, Zelda used a pastry knife to cut a triangle out of it. She bent the triangle into a cone, squeezed it into shape, and poked two holes in its base. "Got your nose," she announced.

Hilda took the nose and pressed it firmly onto the front of a head-shaped mass of dough. She set the head at one end of the linen-covered board and went back to help her sister cut out more body parts. Limb by limb, joint by joint, they assembled a human-shaped, if somewhat flat, figure on the table.

The sisters played silly games as they worked—waggling freshly shaped ears, walking dough-feet to their place on the board, and doing a high five with floury hand shapes—until finally their work was done.

"There," said Zelda, admiring the fruits of their

labor. Then she noticed that something wasn't quite right. "Wait. One arm looks shorter than the other. Hilda, have you been eating dough?"

Hilda looked up like a deer caught in headlights. Her cheeks bulged like a chipmunk's, and there was a snowfall of flour on her chin. "Doh," she lied.

Zelda crossed over to the line of bottles. She set a ceramic bowl on the island. "Now for the personality glaze."

Hilda swallowed loudly, then said, "Pour it on." She reached for a bottle with a label showing footprints in several positions linked by dotted lines. "Let's make him a great dancer." She unstoppered the bottle and poured about an ounce into the bowl. The liquid hit the bowl and skittered around with a brisk tap-dancing sound.

"And a daredevil." Zelda uncorked a red bottle, and an ounce of bubbly liquid jetted up in a graceful arc, looped the loop, and landed in the dead center of the bowl.

Hilda poured out a dollop of bluesy cream flecked with improv that sparkled electrically. "And a musician."

"Do girls still like musicians?" Zelda wondered.

Hilda sniffed scornfully. "Ever since Mozart's 'Feel the Heat' tour." Unfortunately she paid more attention to lecturing Zelda than to the bottle she was pouring from at the time. When she looked back, the rose-colored bottle of bubbly liquid was half empty. "Uh-oh. I think I overdid the enthusiasm."

Zelda pooh-poohed her concern. "He's going to a high school dance. He's going to need all the enthusiasm he can get." She stirred the mixture vigorously for a few minutes, then took the bowl over to the dough man. Hilda handed her one of a pair of wide pastry brushes, and they began spreading the glaze over the flat figure.

When the bowl was empty, Hilda covered the dough with a sheet and Zelda set a kitchen timer. Within minutes the shape under the sheet began to rise, and rich odors filled the house.

The odd aroma caught Sabrina's attention, and she came downstairs to the kitchen with a puzzled expression. "What are you cooking? Something smells"—she groped for an appropriate description—"handsome?"

Zelda wiped her hands on a towel and announced proudly, "Sabrina, you're going to love it! We're making you a dream date—out of Man-Doh." She handed Sabrina the box.

"Man-Doh?" The name sounded strange, and the large box with its homey red type looked out of place. Sabrina had never imagined ready-to-use packaged spells.

"He'll be tall, dark, and yeasty," enthused Hilda.

"Now, he'll last about four hours," explained Zelda, "which is perfect for your dance."

Sabrina was left almost speechless by the way her aunts just didn't *get* it. "Yeah, perfect," she groused. "Except that I wanted to go with Harvey, not Poppin' Fresh!"

"Now, just meet him before you make up your mind," Zelda said as she sat Sabrina down on a stool in front of the island.

"You'll like him," said Hilda. "He's *really* enthusiastic."

"I've already made up my mind," Sabrina said firmly. "I'm not going to the dance."

The figure under the sheet swelled upward just as the timer went off with a sharp *ting!*

Zelda and Hilda grinned like schoolgirls, leaning over the sheet-covered form and crying in unison, "Man's done!"

The figure on the board snapped into a sitting position, knocking the sheet away. Sabrina gasped. Her aunts might have started out with water and flour, but what they had turned out was pure beefcake.

He was at least six feet tall. Tight dark curls capped a lean, rugged face. Soulful brown eyes gleamed out from under eyebrows shaped like surprised checkmarks. He had a long, muscular frame and was dressed in a leather jacket over a shirt and jeans—all faded and worn just enough. He looked around as if seeing the world for the very first time—which, of course, he was. He was thrilled to bits. "Hey! Hi! Man, am I happy to be here!" He just radiated enthusiasm.

Sabrina's jaw dropped. "Wow! He is really *cute!*"

Zelda folded her hands and looked prim. "Well, we do nice work. But . . . if you don't want to go to the dance . . ."

119

Sabrina moved over to the French doors, never taking her eyes off the young man on the table. "Changed my mind. I'll go. Just give me a sec to get ready." She waved her finger over her body. Her sweatshirt and jeans were instantly replaced by a crisp black dress with a blue midriff. "All set. Gotta go."

Sabrina grabbed her dream date by the hand and pulled him through the French doors. He followed her, gawking excitedly at everything. "Man! You look great! And this dance sounds fantastic!"

Hilda watched them leave and sighed, feeling the tingle of romance in the air. "I wish they could bottle that kind of enthusiasm." She did a double take. "Oh, wait . . . they did."

# Chapter 14

☆

I know I screamed the whole way, but I actually had fun riding on your motorcycle," said Sabrina as she and her dream date walked through the school toward the cafeteria. A throbbing bass rhythm rattled the lockers in the hallway. "You want your jacket back?"

"No," he said, "it fits you perfectly!"

Sabrina shrugged off the jacket and folded it over her arm. "Actually, it's a little big. We can leave it at the coat check."

Her date was already ahead of her, holding open the double doors to the cafeteria and staring in joyous wonder at everything inside. "This place is fantastic! What do you call it?"

Sabrina looked around. All she could see was a room painted in flat institutional colors and, lately, tricked out with rather cheap-looking paper streamers, bunting, and colored balloons. "The cafeteria?" she answered.

"Cafeteria. I'll have to remember that." He frowned in concentration. Then the decorations caught his eye. "Whoa—great bunting!"

Sabrina started to squirm. "Could you keep it down? You're talking kind of loud."

Jenny came dancing across the room toward them. Unlike all the others on the dance floor, Jenny wasn't dancing with a partner—she was flying solo. She swayed and bounced to the music, her red curls floating over a wine-dark velvet dress. The song ended just as she reached them. "Hi!" she said happily.

"Hi!" bubbled Sabrina, hardly able to contain herself.

"Hi! Who are you?" Sabrina's date asked Jenny.

"I'm Jenny. Who are you?"

The date's jaw hung open, and he turned to Sabrina for help. Sabrina chewed air for a moment. "This is . . ." she began, her mind racing. "Chad . . . Corey . . . Dylan?"

"Great name," said Jenny, impressed.

"Thanks," Sabrina said before she could stop herself. Jenny shot her a funny look, but was obviously twitching to talk. Sabrina caught her date's eye. "Uh . . . Chad, could you go get us some punch?"

Chad was stunned and amazed, as if Sabrina had just performed a miracle. Pointing at Sabrina, he said to Jenny, "She has the *best* ideas!" He dashed off to find refreshments.

Sabrina immediately huddled into chat zone with Jenny. "So what do you think?"

Jenny was flushed with awe. "He's cute. Where did you meet him?"

"My aunts introduced us. We rode over on his mo-tor-cy-cle." Sabrina rolled the syllables out for their fullest effect.

"I approve!" declared Jenny, nodding sharply.

Sabrina beamed coyly. "Yeah. Chad's pretty neat, you know, for an athlete-daredevil-rock musician."

Jenny's eyes widened.

Chad came gliding up holding a cup in one hand, his other hand behind his back. "Guess what? They have *two* flavors—orange . . ." He thrust the cup toward Sabrina, then whipped another cup out from behind his back like a magician performing a trick. "And red!"

Sabrina took the red drink from Chad's hand. Chad tasted his orange drink, then beamed with pleasure and chugged the rest.

"Go easy, Chad," Sabrina cautioned. "It's early."

The music started up again, and the floor began to fill up with couples. Jenny looked around nervously for a moment, then firmed her jaw and announced to Sabrina and Chad, "Well, I'm going to dance." She moved toward the middle of the floor.

Chad was dumbfounded by this option. "Wait a second—we can *dance* here?"

"Yeah," said Sabrina. "Do you like to dance?"

"I'm *made* to dance! And I *love* this song!" Chad scooped the drink cup out of Sabrina's hand. He spun around to press the two cups into the hands of the nearest person. "Here, excuse me—hold this. Thanks a lot!" He escorted Sabrina onto the dance floor.

He was as good as his word. Sabrina thought about it and realized that in Chad's case, saying he was made to dance was the literal truth. He moved with a loose-limbed ease that distracted her from the crispness of his steps. He made dancing look as simple as breathing.

As Sabrina and Chad floated over the dance floor, a very annoyed Libby Chessler stalked into the cafeteria, with a glum Harvey Kinkle trailing a foot or two behind her. Libby marched over to confront her lackey, Sasha, at the refreshment table. "Sasha, what have I missed?" she demanded.

"Not much. Where have you been?"

Harvey wriggled with embarrassment. "We had some engine trouble with the Vette on the way over."

Sasha's eyes widened. "You drive a Corvette?"

Libby corrected her archly: "That's *Che*-vette."

"Hey, same manufacturer," Harvey said defensively.

"Oh, please," Libby said frostily, annoyed at

how thick Harvey could be. And Sasha wasn't much swifter. If the airheaded novice cheerleader didn't make such a loyal follower, Libby would have ditched her in a minute. Then her searching glare found Sabrina and her date. "Omigod," she suddenly gasped. "Who's the guy Sabrina's with?"

Jenny came dancing by. "His name's Chad Corey Dylan. And, yes, that's his motorcycle outside," she taunted.

Sasha threw up her hands. "Well, I guess Sabrina wins," she chirped.

Libby's face was set in a grim mask. "I don't think so," she hissed through clenched teeth. Then her stage presence reasserted itself. "Come on, Harvey, let's hit the floor!"

Harvey's grip on Libby's arm stopped her cold. He smiled sheepishly at her and said, "Actually, Libby, I don't dance."

The simple statement hit Libby like a slap in the face. She stepped forward to stare at Harvey eye to eye. "Ex*cuse* me? This is a *dance*. Guess what we *do* here."

Harvey squirmed. "Well, see, for me 'dance' is sort of a metaphor." His hands made vague circling gestures.

"For what?" Libby asked coldly.

"I don't know . . . something else?"

Libby pressed forward, backing Harvey up against the row of chairs by the wall. He tumbled backward into a seat. "I can't believe you did this to me," Libby growled. She skewered him with a lethal look and then snapped her fingers. "Sasha. Ladies' room."

She turned and stormed out, leaving Sasha to catch up.

Even Libby's venom couldn't have dented Chad's aura of enthusiasm. He flashed perfect white teeth at Sabrina. "Man, I'm having a great time!" he said happily, swinging Sabrina around.

"Me, too." Sabrina beamed. But switching positions with Chad brought Harvey into view. He was sitting dejectedly on the sidelines. Seeing Sabrina, he gave her a weak little wave. All vitality faded from the music, and the colorful bunting paled. Sabrina stood still.

Chad kept moving but asked in confusion, "Hey, why'd you stop dancing?"

Sabrina forced a smile. "I just saw someone," she said.

"Who?"

A feeling of dismay almost choked Sabrina as she said sadly, "Just a friend."

☆

# Chapter 15

☆

The Spellman kitchen table supported two large boards, side by side. On each board lay a linen-draped man-shape, rising slowly. Zelda and Hilda sat on stools at the island, reading to pass the time until their dates were ready. Zelda was flipping through the latest issue of *Scientific American* while Hilda drooled over Delilah Van Loockenblush's latest potboiler, *The Bodice Ripp'd*. Hilda kept peeking over her book at the table. She fidgeted in anticipation. "This is fun. We haven't done this since the Taft administration."

Without raising her eyes from her magazine, Zelda nodded in agreement. "What did you put in your personality?" she asked.

Hilda clutched her book to her chest and smiled dreamily. "I gave him *lots* of optimism. I want my dream date to be hopeful."

"Oh, that's nice," Zelda murmured.

*Ting!* the timer rang. "Mine's done!" shouted Hilda.

The first date pulled his sheet off and sat up. He was a burly blond with biceps almost as big as his head. Hilda sat on the board beside him and leaned in close. "Hi," she said brightly. "I'm Hilda. You're Simon."

Simon scowled without looking at Hilda. "Would you get off my back?" he complained. "I've been *looking* for work. Stop *riding* me!"

Zelda put down her magazine, concerned. "That doesn't sound too hopeful."

Simon still hadn't looked at Hilda. He simply sat on the board with a brooding expression. Hilda studied him closely. "Something must have gone wrong," she said.

"Did you check the expiration date on the optimism?"

Hilda hopped off the table and ran to check the label on the bottle. "Oh, no. It says, 'Hope fades.'"

"Which means . . ."

Hilda stared glumly at the glowering Simon. "My dream date is hopeless!"

"Ladies," said Simon, hopping off the table to tower over the sisters. "You want to break up the hen party? Somewhere men are competing in a professional sport, and I'm missing it. So where's the TV? Never mind. I'll find it myself." He left the kitchen.

Hilda was disappointed and furious at the same

time. "I have the worst luck with men! Even the ones made out of dough!"

Zelda picked up the rolling pin and held it out. "Here—you want to start over?"

"Yes. No. Wait, I have an idea." Hilda's face lit up. "Maybe I can *change* him."

Zelda groaned, "Oh, Hilda, you know that never works."

"But I love a challenge," Hilda said. Schemes filled her mind. "First I'll gain his trust by pretending to be interested in sports." She headed toward the parlor.

"Wait," Zelda called. "Don't you even want to see who my dream date is?"

Hilda paused at the door, seemingly annoyed at being sidetracked by so trivial a matter. "Let me guess. He's a brave, milk-swilling fireman."

Zelda's face fell. "How did you know?"

"I found the *Baywatch Nights* calendar in your desk." When Hilda saw her sister's shock, she added, "Sabrina's right—there is no privacy in this house." Then she sped out of the kitchen.

*Ting!* cried the timer again. Zelda turned in time to watch the unveiling of her dream date. A compact, handsome man in a bright yellow fireman's jacket sat up and smiled at her. "Oh, hello, kitten. Got milk?" With dark hair and twinkling eyes, he was a dead ringer for Eddie Cibrian.

"Mee-ow, Darryl," purred Zelda.

"What?" Salem poked his head out of the picnic basket. Zelda and Darryl ignored him. "Oh, sorry," the cat said. "Thought you were talking to me." He slid back down into the dark warmth.

Chad's endurance on the dance floor was far more impressive than Sabrina's. This was their sixth straight number, and Sabrina was starting to wilt, but Chad just kept bopping along. "Oh, man!" he'd say from time to time. "This is the greatest night of my life!"

Sabrina slowed to a halt. "Look, I'm sorta tired. You mind if I take a breather?"

"No," said Chad agreeably. "Although I've gotta say, I *love* this song!"

"Then keep dancing," Sabrina insisted. She snagged Jenny from the dance floor. "Jenny, cover for me," she hissed and shoved the redheaded girl into position in front of the gyrating Chad.

Jenny was caught between principle and loyalty. "All right. But don't be long. I don't want people thinking I sold out."

Sabrina was already at the refreshment table. Harvey, his face intense with concentration, was swirling a ladle around in the punch bowl. The red flavor. Sabrina threw him a quick smile. "Hi, Harvey. Are you busy?"

"Uh, no. I dropped a chip in the punch." He gave up on his search and glanced shyly down at Sabrina. "You look nice," he said.

"Thanks. You do, too."

"Really?" said Harvey, surprised. He looked down at his long gray zip-up vest, black sweatshirt, and jeans. "This is what I wore to school yesterday."

Sabrina shrugged. "Yeah, well, you smell okay. So where's Libby?"

"Bathroom, I guess." Harvey ducked his head. "She's mad at me because I don't dance."

That surprised Sabrina. "Really? I would have thought you'd be good at that."

Harvey screwed up his face, struggling to find the right words to express his feelings. "I'm okay when it's just me rocking out in my room," he confessed. "I mean, I don't spin around a pole or anything. But I get really self-conscious in front of other people."

Sabrina rolled her eyes. "We *all* do."

"Not your date." Harvey nodded his head toward the dance floor, where Chad was dancing rings around Jenny.

Now it was Sabrina's turn to find a way to explain. Or *not* explain, actually. "Well, Chad's kinda special," she said.

Harvey's face sagged a little, and he looked away from Sabrina. "You really like him, don't you?"

Sabrina suddenly caught Harvey's reading of the word "special." "No, I meant—"

A bobbing body like a marionette on musical strings came between them. "There you are!" cried Chad, turning to Sabrina. He executed a quick step-shuffle-ball-change and then a dip, finishing off with a hand extended to Harvey. "Hi, I'm Chad Corey Dylan."

Harvey automatically shook his hand. Even shaking hands, Chad kept rhythm to the music, tugging Harvey's hand back and forth. "Hi. I'm Harvey. Dwight. Kinkle."

"Great to meet you!" Chad smiled as he took Sabrina by the arm. "Come on, Sabrina, you wouldn't believe what you're missing."

"A great song?" cracked Sabrina.

Chad rocked back with astonishment. "You know *everything!*" He glowed as he pulled her toward the dance floor.

Harvey poked around in the punch bowl some more until Libby and Sasha returned. "You're back," he greeted them. "I thought maybe you'd fallen in."

Libby was underwhelmed by his wit. "Charming," she sneered.

Hilda batted her blue eyes at Simon. She was curled up next to him on the living room couch. Leaning close and smiling attentively like a puppy, she was the perfect picture of feminine subservience. "What are you thinking?" she murmured.

None of this had the slightest effect on Simon. His eyes were locked on the TV screen. "That ref's a *jerk*," he said in rising irritation at the quality of play.

If Hilda was anything, she was persistent. "You know, we could *talk* while we watch sports." She snuggled closer. "I mean, relationships *are* built on communication. Why don't you share your feel-ings?"

Simon stared at her in disbelief. "Why don't you share the chips?" was his only reply.

"Simon, the point I'm trying to make is—"

"Look, look. When we get to a boring commer-cial, we'll make out. Until then . . ." He gestured toward the TV. "Ya mind?"

In the kitchen, Zelda was discovering the short-comings of a personality with brush-on depth. "I've never seen a man drink so much milk."

Darryl had just finished chugging his third quart. "Ahh," he said, smacking his lips, "I like milk." Then he sat still, smiling quietly at Zelda.

Zelda tried to get the ball rolling again. "So what should we do now?"

Darryl thought. "Checkers?"

"No." This was going nowhere fast.

Darryl thought again. "Parcheesi?"

"No." Dead stop.

"Want me to rescue the cat again?"

"No!" yowled Salem, skidding on the floor as he ran away.

It was a night when none of them seemed happy with their dates. "I don't understand why you didn't just say no when I asked you to this dance," Libby growled at Harvey.

"I told you—I'm working on it," Harvey said as

he winced and looked away. Libby's glares could singe eyebrows.

The music shifted rhythm, slowing to half the heart rate of the rocking crowd. Out on the floor, couples moved closer as the lights dimmed.

"All right! A slow dance!" Whatever the speed, whatever the melody, Chad threw himself into it. He reached for Sabrina.

She held an arm between them. "You know," she said, "I'm not really into slow dances. Why don't we go stand over by those chairs."

Chad responded as if this were the best suggestion he'd ever heard. "Genius, just genius!" he crowed. Sabrina smiled and led the way toward the wall.

All alone in a sea of couples, Jenny tried to stick it out. She closed her eyes and swayed to the music, but a shiver ran through her. "This is too weird— even for me," she finally decided and fled the floor.

Libby was slumped in a chair next to Harvey, radiating barely suppressed fury as Sabrina and Chad headed their way. "If you don't want to be here, just leave," Libby hissed at Harvey.

"Look," Harvey began. "I don't tell many people this, but—"

"There he is!" Libby interrupted, leaping out of her chair at the sight of Chad approaching. She snapped to a stop a foot away from Sabrina's date. Sabrina, she completely ignored. "Hi. I'm Libby."

"Hi, I'm Chad." He offered his hand, glad to meet anybody.

Libby faked a blush. "Saw you dancing out there. You're really good."

"Oh, well, I'm also a daredevil and a rock musician." Modesty was obviously not one of the ingredients in his personality glaze.

It wasn't one of Libby's natural ingredients either. She was majorly impressed. "Really? What instrument do you play?"

Chad shrugged and folded his arms. "Lead guitar," he said smugly.

"Mmph," snorted Harvey, getting up from his chair. "Lead guitar . . ."

Sabrina moved quickly to bring him into the conversation. "Hey, Harvey," she said, "don't you play an instrument?"

"Yeah. The bassoon." Harvey beamed at the mention of his favorite instrument.

"Wow. The bassoon," Sabrina said brightly. "I think that's really sexy."

"Maybe to another bassoon." Libby commented scornfully.

The slow dance music ended and a staccato guitar riff announced the next number. Chad, of course, was stoked. "Oh, man, I *love* this song!"

"Me, too," added Libby quickly. She turned to frown at Harvey. "Unfortunately, *my* date can't dance."

"Yes, he can," Sabrina protested. "As a matter of fact, Harvey is a wonderful dancer."

Harvey hated these complex moments. "Sabrina," he said, *"technically* that's not true."

"Yes, it is," Sabrina insisted. She crossed her arms and grinned at him. "Why don't you prove it? Now." Under cover of her arms, Sabrina flicked a finger at Harvey. A bright spark flew through the air faster than sight.

Harvey suddenly spun in place, snapping his arms high and ending *en pointe*. He balanced perfectly for a moment and then slowly sank back on his heels. "Okay," he admitted, shucking his vest. "Maybe I know a *few* steps."

He sailed out onto the floor, backstepping in time to the music, the taps on his shoes accenting some jazzy footwork. The other teenagers pulled back to clear a circle around him. Harvey improvised a set that combined tap, jazz, some ballet, and a healthy dose of Broadway flash. He pirouetted, breaking the spin with stag leaps and a *ciseaux,* a scissorlike jump, before ending with a high jump that brought him back down *en demi-pointe.*

Jenny was thrilled by his performance and used it to validate her own unconventional position. "Hey! Harvey's dancing alone!" she crowed to her stunned classmates.

Sabrina was impressed as well. Her magic spark had only been intended to overcome Harvey's reluctance to dance. The skill he displayed was all his. "He's actually better than Chad."

"Much better!" Chad admitted.

Harvey held his final pose for a moment and then slowly became aware that he was the center of attention. He ducked his head and slunk back to his friends. "Did anyone see that?" he asked anxiously.

Libby beamed at him. Once again he was a prize in her eyes. *"Everyone* saw it."

Harvey tried to shrink inside himself. "Now I feel really self-conscious," he moaned.

Sabrina had no chance to console him. Chad scooped her up by the waist and almost dragged her onto the floor. "Let's dance. I feel inspired!"

"I think I'd better go," Harvey told Libby, not meeting her eyes.

"What?" Libby was shocked. "I want to dance with you now."

"Sorry, Libby," Harvey mumbled. "You said I could leave if I wanted to."

"I take it back," Libby snapped furiously. "You *have* to dance with me."

"Libby . . ." Harvey began. He waved his hand uncertainly between them. Then his body stiffened with resolve. He pointed his index finger firmly at Libby. "No," he said with conviction. Then he bolted from the room.

Sabrina saw Harvey leave and stopped dancing. "Look, Chad," she said. "This doesn't feel right. Excuse me, I gotta go." She headed for the door.

"Harvey? Harvey?" Sabrina called as she left the school building. Harvey was nowhere in sight. "Harvey?" she called again.

"I'm over here," came a voice from behind Sabrina.

She turned and saw Harvey sitting dejectedly on

a bench near the door. "I thought you were leaving."

Harvey's face twisted wryly. "Yeah, well, I wanted to, but now I have to wait for Triple-A."

"I could help you wait. I'm good at that. Watch." Sabrina went over and sat beside him.

"Thanks." Harvey shrugged. "But shouldn't you be inside with What's-his-name What's-his-name What's-his-name?"

"No. He's not really my type."

"What? 'Perfect' isn't your type?"

Sabrina fidgeted uncomfortably. The moment to really communicate with Harvey had finally come. "Actually, Harvey, I wanted to talk to you about that. But it's kind of hard for me." She stood up with her back to Harvey. Her resolve was weakening.

"What do you mean?"

Sabrina walked to the other side of the entranceway. "Well, the thing is . . . I . . . see . . ."

"Sabrina, what is it?" Harvey got up and started to walk toward her.

"Freeze!" Sabrina commanded, pointing a finger at Harvey. He stopped in his tracks like a statue, one leg straight and the other in midstep. Despite his awkward position, he didn't fall over.

With Harvey immobilized, Sabrina felt free to talk. "The thing is, I came to this dance expecting to have a good time with Chad. But . . . one look at you and it was over. I mean, it's nice that we're friends, but sometimes I wish it were more." She looked longingly at the tall, handsome boy. "I like you, Harvey. I like you a lot. But I guess for now this is the closest I can get to saying it to your face."

Sabrina fell silent, staring into Harvey's unseeing eyes. "Thanks for listening."

She flicked a finger and Harvey resumed motion. He blinked and seemed confused. "Did you just say something?" he asked.

Sabrina was quick to cover her tracks. "Yeah. I said, uh, Chad isn't really perfect. You know, one arm's longer than the other. Well, I'd better get back." She headed for the door.

Harvey cleared his throat and took a hesitant step forward to cut her off. "Sabrina? I was wondering . . . since we're out here . . . do you wanna dance?"

Sabrina's heart pounded. Was Harvey suggesting an action? On his own? Or could his subconscious have heard what Sabrina said while he was frozen? She smiled, just in case it was a joke. "Won't you feel self-conscious?"

Harvey shrugged. "It's just us."

He took her right hand in his left and slid his other arm around her waist. Even though muffled by brick walls, the music in the cafeteria was loud enough to provide a soft accompaniment to their dance. They circled each other gracefully.

This was more than Sabrina had ever hoped for. Her spirit soared and gave wings to their dance. It felt more like an old-time musical number than real life. They pulled apart, arms spread, hanging on by only their fingertips. Tongue in cheek, Sabrina asked, "So do you love this song?"

Harvey snorted. " 'Sokay."

He spun her back into his arms. Sabrina could feel his heartbeat against her back. Then she felt Harvey grow tense. "Uh-oh. I'm starting to get self-conscious."

She spun in his arms again and this time let herself sink backward, forcing Harvey to follow her dip. Their eyes met and held.

A flush crept over Harvey's cheeks. "Okay, I'm there," he said, and straightened up. He held Sabrina at arm's length and shrugged. "Sorry. That's all I can do."

Sabrina smiled. "It was enough. I think I'm ready to go home now."

Harvey brightened. "Hey, if you're done with the dance, you want to go over to the Slicery and play a little Foosball?" The very suggestion of being somewhere other than at the dance loosened Harvey up.

His enthusiasm was infectious. Sabrina gave a little leap and said, "Yeah! I love Foosball!" She did a rueful double take at her behavior. "Sorry. I've been hanging out with Chad too long. I'll go tell him that I'm leaving."

Harvey watched Sabrina skip lightly up the steps and disappear into the school. "I like you, Sabrina," he said, his lips barely moving. A shiver ran through him, and he turned away, annoyed at himself. "Why can't I say it to her face?"

Sabrina skirted the edge of the dance floor, dodging around a few of her fellow students who were a little bit off in their sense of where the "dance" part of the floor ended. Chad caught sight of her and leaped up from his chair. "Sabrina, you're back!"

Sabrina didn't relish what she had to do now, but she couldn't think of any way around it. "Chad, we need to talk. It was sweet of you to take me to this dance, but you're not the one I want to be with." There, it was out in the open now.

Chad asked her in utter seriousness, "Well, who do you want to be with?"

Sabrina flinched. She wasn't going to get off the hook so easily. She was going to have to tell him the truth. "Harvey."

Chad's face lit up. He stuck his hand out to shake Sabrina's. "That's an excellent choice. He's a great guy!"

Sabrina was floored. "You really *are* a dream date, Chad. So it's okay that I'm leaving?"

Chad crossed his arms and tried to look self-sufficient. "Sure—go ahead. I'll just stay here and miss you."

That one stung Sabrina. "I don't want you to do that." She kicked her brain into gear. "Look, you only have two hours left, and I'm sure you love this song, so why not ask Libby to dance?"

It was Chad's turn to be floored. "Can I? I like Libby," he confessed.

"You *like* Libby?" Sabrina tried not to look horrified.

Chad shrugged. "Sorry. I guess I'm starting to go bad."

Sabrina gave him a quick hug before he strolled over to where Libby was sitting alone. She watched the cheerleader's expression shift into the adoring gaze of a puppy when Chad asked her to dance. Satisfied, she left.

Harvey was sitting on the bench when Sabrina came back outside. She struck a pose of challenge. "All right. Foos it or lose it."

"Hey, look," Harvey said, holding his arms out before him. "Same length. Hah!"

Sabrina wet her finger and made a score mark in the air. They laughed all the way to the Slicery.

Back at the Spellman house, Hilda was having difficulty scoring. Her brain hurt from the effort to understand how the players on the TV screen knew what they were doing. "So if you live by the pass, you die by the pass," she recited. "They kept the ball on the ground, and they were able to convert in the red zone."

She sat back, unsure if her latest tactic would have any effect on Simon. The game wasn't due back on for another few minutes, so this was her only chance. To her surprise, Simon turned to her.

"You know, I can't hear Pat Summerall while you're yappin'," he said, flapping his hand like a beak at her.

"This is a hardware commercial."

Simon put a finger to his lips and urged respect. "Shhh! He's talking about hammers."

Hilda stood up, disgusted. "Okay, that's it!" She stormed into the kitchen, making a direct line for the island. She ducked around Darryl, who was climbing into his yellow plastic gear at top speed. "Coming through," she barked.

"Done!" Darryl shouted.

Zelda pushed the stem of the stopwatch in her hand. "Nineteen seconds!" she crowed. Darryl relaxed. It had taken him ten tries, but he'd finally made good on his boast to be ready to roll in twenty seconds or less.

Hilda snatched up the rolling pin and stalked back to the parlor. "Be back in a jiff."

Zelda ignored her sister. She lounged on the table, staring dreamily at her fireman pinup. "So what now?" she asked in a throaty voice.

Darryl thought hard. "Well, I can register your bike or make lasagna for fifty."

"Could you teach me the Heimlich maneuver?"

"Sure," he said. Zelda slid off the table. But Darryl was heading for the refrigerator again.

"First, I need a milk break to fortify my body and build healthy teeth and bones."

As Zelda sighed and watched Darryl pour himself yet another tumbler of milk, Hilda came back into the kitchen, struggling under the weight of a huge lump of dough. Hilda stepped on the garbage-can pedal and tossed the lump in when the lid opened. She dusted off her hands. "Yes! I finally got through to Simon." She turned to Darryl, grinned, and snuggled up alongside him. "Well, since my dream date turned out to be a dud, I guess we'll just have to share yours, Zelda." She dug her fingers into Darryl's arm.

"Oh, no!" Zelda snagged Darryl's other arm, the one with the glass of milk. "I'm not sharing. He's mine."

"Be nice," Hilda whined, tugging the arm she'd snuggled up to.

Zelda tightened her own grip and pulled Darryl back. "I made him. Let go."

"I won't!" Hilda said, yanking Darryl's arm as hard as she could.

With the soft sound of dough parting, the arm holding the milk glass came off in Zelda's hand, yellow sleeve and all. "*Now* look what you've done!"

Darryl was horror-struck. He stared at his lost limb. "My milk . . ." he whimpered.

Hilda smiled pleadingly at her sister. "He's damaged now. Can I have him?"

\* \* \*

On their way back from the Slicery, Sabrina and Harvey peeped in the window of the cafeteria to see how Chad was doing with Libby. The glass was clear enough to see him still bopping away. They didn't even have to read lips well to know he was saying, "Oh, man, I *love* this song!"

Libby felt that all eyes must be on her and her *superlative* partner. She radiated pride and superiority. "You and I are so right for each other," she crowed.

She spun and faced the other way to see who was watching from that angle. Suddenly Chad doubled over. He coughed, and flour flew from his lips. He staggered toward the doors. "Must . . . find . . . preservatives," he gasped.

Libby spun back around and discovered that her dance partner was gone. "Chad? Chad?" she called. She walked swiftly across the dance floor, seeing no trace of Chad. He wasn't anywhere to be found. She ran out the front door of the school, calling, "Chad?"

Chad had vanished. Libby strode into the darkness, hoping for a glimpse of her dream date. But all she found was a moist mass of dough that clung to her shoe when she stepped in it. "Eww. Oh, gross!" she said, flinching and twitching in disgust. She scraped her feet off on the brick edging of the lawn and then ran for the phones.

The last Sabrina and Harvey saw of Libby, she was arguing on the phone. "Are you a detective?"

they heard her say. "Okay, I'd like to report a missing person. Chad Corey Dylan. Well, he's really tall and really cute. Oh, sorry. Specifically, I'd say he's six-two, blue eyes, short dark hair. And he's super-enthusiastic. He was last seen dancing with me, and everyone was looking. It was *so* cool. . . . What? Well, he's only been gone twenty minutes, but I'm not going to wait twenty-four hours! Don't you get it? This is the love of my life! Hello? Hello . . .?"

Harvey and Sabrina melted silently into the night.

Sabrina came strolling into the house just in time to see Darryl lose his arm in the tug-of-war between the Spellman sisters. Her aunts immediately stopped struggling and tried to compose themselves. "What's up?" Sabrina asked with a twinkle in her eye.

"Not much," said Hilda, as nonchalantly as she could, considering she was still clutching Darryl's remaining arm. "How was your dream date?"

"Great. Harvey and I ditched the dance and went to the Slicery to play Foosball."

"Harvey?" Zelda asked in surprise. "What happened to the date we made for you?"

"Chad? I gave him to Libby," Sabrina said offhandedly.

"You gave Libby your dream date? That makes

no sense." Zelda screwed up her face at the thought.

"Neither does a one-armed fireman, but you don't see *me* grilling *you*." Sabrina started up the steps, smiling. "*I* respect *your* privacy. Good night."

# Epilogue

☆

☆

It was well past midnight, but it was a weekend and Sabrina couldn't sleep. Thinking that he was keeping her company, Salem had launched into a detailed recitation of his plans for world conquest. Sabrina didn't mind. The cat's monologue provided a comforting backdrop for her own thoughts. She sat on her bed, idly thumbing through her magic book and sipping from a glass of milk.

In her few short weeks at Westbridge, Sabrina's life had turned upside down and inside out. She wasn't who she thought she was. Not only did she have to cope with a new school and a new town, but she was just beginning to realize how much she would have to change if she hoped to become a practicing, safety-conscious witch.

Magic could do a lot of unbelievable things. She had seen that for herself. There were also a lot of things it couldn't do. It could also do a great deal of harm, as she had discovered the hard way.

But she realized that she would never even consider going back to the way she was before. Before Zelda and Hilda. Before Jenny and Harvey. Especially Harvey. The completely natural magic glow from their brief dance together still clung to her, lifting her spirits and promising more joys to be found in the future.

She had even come to appreciate the obnoxious, self-centered, egomaniacal Salem, the poor would-be witch-king of the world. He was digging his claws into the comforter as he happily outlined his scenario for world domination. Sabrina drank the last of her milk as he droned on.

"And once I controlled Eurasia, I was going to advance on the little con—"

"Uh, Salem, can you hold that thought?" Sabrina interrupted. "I'll be right back. I've gotta get some more milk."

"Stay where you are," Salem said. "You're a witch. Look under *M.*"

Sabrina flipped through the great book. She ran her finger down the appropriate page. "Wow. 'Magic milk.'" She pointed her finger at her glass. Slowly, steadily, the level of the white liquid in the glass rose. "Cool. It worked! I could get used to this magic."

*Yes, I could,* she thought. *I could get used to it indeed.*

# About the Authors

DAVID CODY WEISS and BOBBI JG WEISS are writing partners. They're also married. And they have lots of cats. Day after day they slog away at their computers, racking their brains to write up fanciful and often absurd stories that they then sell to publishers. They have written a whole lot of stuff, including novels *(Are You Afraid of the Dark?: The Tale of the Shimmering Shell; The Secret World of Alex Mack: Close Encounters; Star Trek TNG: Starfleet Academy: Breakaway; Star Trek Voyager: Starfleet Academy: Lifeline)*, novel adaptations *(Jingle All the Way)*, comic books *(Pinky and the Brain; Animaniacs)*, trading cards *(Batman and Robin, Star Trek Universe, James Bond Connoisseur Collection)*, and other weird stuff like clothing tag blurbs, office catalog copy, and little squeezy books for kids who can't read yet so they just look at the pictures and squeeze the squeezy toy.

Bobbi and David hope to be filthy rich one day because laughing all the way to the bank sounds like fun.

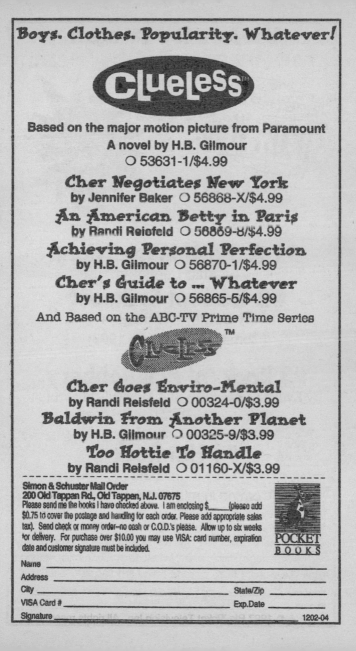